NEW FRONTIER

---THE FIVE BRATS---

GABE ROMERO

authorHOUSE®

AuthorHouse™
1663 Liberty Drive
Bloomington, IN 47403
www.authorhouse.com
Phone: 1 (800) 839-8640

Published by AuthorHouse 09/03/2015

ISBN: 978-1-5049-2540-2 (sc)
ISBN: 978-1-5049-2539-6 (e)

Library of Congress Control Number: 2015912040

Print information available on the last page.

C O N T E N T S

ROMERISCOPE PRODUCTIONS PRESENTS A GABRIEL E. RODRIGUEZ PRODUCTION "NEW FRONTIER: THE FIVE BRATS" STARRING GABE ROMERO – TERRY FARRAN – BRIAN RENDETTI – RANDY PICKINGS – BILLY FONDER – LAUREN STONE – MEGHAN OVERBAY – JOSH DISINELL – STACEY NORTON – GENERAL CUE AND CAPTAIN KRISTINA PORTER AS HERSELF SPECIAL APPEARANCES BY ADMIRALS JUSTIN AMAYA – CASEY RUSTIN AND PRESIDENT LARRY FISCHER AND A SPECIAL CAMEO APPEARANCE BY BROOKE TAYLOR BASED UPON THE HUMOR OF GABRIEL E RODRIGUEZ PRODUCED BY THE ROMERO FOUNDATION EDITORS GABRIEL E RODRIGUEZ AND MIKE REEVES PRODUCTION DESIGNER YOUR IMAGINATION, INC. CAMERAS BY MORE OF YOUR IMAGINATION, A SUBSIDARY OF YOUR IMAGINATION, INC DIRECTOR OF PHOTOGRAPHY PICTURE IT YOURSELF CO. EXECUTIVE PRODUCER GABE ROMERO COSTUMES BY YOUR THOTS, INCORPORATED WRITTEN BY GABRIEL E RODRIGUEZ PUBLISHED BY NO ONE PUBLISHING COMPANY BASED UPON THE FIVE BRATS CREATED BY GABRIEL E RODRIGUEZ DIRECTED BY GABE ROMERO A ROMERISCOPE PRODUCTIONS RELEASE

| R | For Language, Scenes of Battle & Perilous Content and Strong Sexual Content with a Butt-load of Nudity (Just Kidding) |

CHAPTER 1

- - - - - T H E   M E E T I N G - - - - -

2020 AD...

"What are we doing here?" Gabe Romero asked Randy Pickings as he walked into a conference room that was not well lit. In it contained an ovular conference table with office chairs outlining the perimeter. A podium was located in the spot of the CEO's position, and a huge blackboard was hung on the wall behind the podium.

Gabe and Randy, together with Billy Fonder, Josh Disinell, Terry Farran, Lauren Stone, and Meghan Overbay, walked into the room. As Gabe and Randy walked in front, the rest were following right behind them. They all donned military formal uniforms, that of the United States Marines.

"Well," Randy started, "in case you forgot, the U.S. Marines came to us with an offer. They said to cooperate or be charged with felonies for incidents in our heyday as T5B." Randy was full figured, but not overweight. He was a stocky and broad fellow, with short curly hair and deep inset eyes. He also sported a mustache and goatee.

"Typical blackmail, if you ask me." Gabe said. He was contrary to Randy. He had a very slender frame with a defining muscle tone throughout his body. He normally wore a ball cap, but for this occasion, he gelled his hair and gave the appearance of a seasoned military officer, even though neither he nor his friends were even in any military branch. They only wore these outfits for the benefit of appearance, as suggested by the Marines.

"Well, call it what you want," Randy said back to Gabe.

Gabe straightened his jacket and glanced around, "Where's Brian?"

"Hell if I know," Randy said, noticing the missing person.

Meanwhile, Billy and Josh were having their own conversation behind them. "You know," Josh started, "I was just about to go on vacation in Columbia. I had just bought two cruise tickets."

"What I should be doing is working on my curriculum for next semester." Billy was also slender and looked like a classic nerd out of the 1980's. He sported the new fashion in glasses, though, unlike the nerdy ones that were of the eighties. He taught classes on mechanics of the newly designed solar car. Only recently had the solar car become popular because the advancements in the non-gasoline engine. Josh was a tall fellow, with a little extra weight for a fuller look. He was a drug lord in Lubbock, Texas until he was picked up by the Marines, and thus, to Josh's knowledge, unaware of his current business.

"What the heck is going on?" Lauren asked Meghan on the way in the door.

"I don't know, but these uniforms are uber tight," Meghan said while wiggling in her jacket, adjusting it. Within seconds, everybody reached a chair at the conference table and took their turn to sit down. Even the other military personnel that had walked in as the friends did took their own turns to sit down.

A man with shallow features approached the podium, "Ladies and Gentlemen: may I present Captain Kristina Porter." The military personnel took it upon themselves to stand up formally, as if they were saluting a superior officer. Gabe and the others followed their lead.

Captain Porter approached the podium. She was five-foot ten with curvy features: not too skinny and not too overweight. She was also the same age as

Gabe, who was twenty-nine. "At ease." As everybody sat back down, she continued uninterrupted, "I must remind you, either here in the military or not, this meeting is classified, and any leak outside of this conference room will be considered treason."

Gabe glanced at Randy, ignoring Porter, "Looks a little too young to be Captain."

Randy returned the glance, "Either incredibly smart or incredibly stupid."

Gabe smirked and turned his attention back to the Captain.

"That includes you, Mr. Romero." Porter said with a stern, serious look on her face. Gabe wiped the smirk away from his face and stood formally with the rest of the crew. She continued after a brief pause, "Now that that has been said and clarified, may I present Admiral Casey Rustin."

As she left the podium, Rustin walked from an entrance in the back. Everyone once again stood up and took the proper stance of salutation. Rustin placed the papers he had been carrying in his hand on the podium and straightened them. "As ease," he said, looking up. As everybody sat down, he spoke. "I am going to be blunt with you folks. In roughly a millennium, the ozone layer on earth will be gone completely and we will all die a horrific, painful death. But in such chaos that I am sure is to come, we must celebrate, because today we are in preparation to go to Mars."

Gabe stood up, "What's your point, Admiral?"

Everyone gasped.

"Gabe!" Terry Farran nudged him. He had sat down on Gabe's left, opposite Randy.

"What?" Gabe shrugged, "This doesn't concern us. This is a military operation and doesn't concern us one bit."

"On the contrary," Captain Porter interrupted, "This totally involves you, so *sit down.*"

Gabe, stunned by the order, sat down, biting his lower lip.

"Now that peace had been restored," Rustin continued, "The details for this mission are yet to come, but for the moment, let me introduce the Director of Operations for this mission." He gestured with his hand, not giving any name. Some personnel started to stand up, as if to salute again, but Rustin signaled to the uneasy that it was not necessary and to remain seated.

A man of medium build had walked into the room and in the direction of the podium. As he passed Gabe and the others, he noticed how suddenly their facial expressions changed to a state of shock. The man, dressed in a black trench coat with a suit underneath, reached the podium. He opened his briefcase and pulled out a notebook and placed it on the podium. He then set his briefcase onto the floor, stood straight up and looked at the seven friends.

It was Brian Rendetti.

"Welcome, old, friends," Brian stated, intentionally pausing between each word. Perhaps it was for emphasis, perhaps not, but with the smirk hiding underneath his tone, everyone took it as so.

Gabe immediately jumped out of seat. "What is the meaning of this?" He had burst out and slammed his hands flat down on the table.

"Sit down, Mr. Romero." Porter interrupted, warning him.

He glared at her for a few moments, contemplating her orders. He then looked at Randy, who gave him a nod. He sat back down, clenching his jaw. Brian ignored the outburst, and once peace had been restored, he looked in the direction of his friends, if that is what one would call them to him, and spoke.

"T5B, or also known as, The Five Brats," Brian started. "Several years ago, five friends set off

4

on terrorizing, 'playing' with, and helping other people in the city of Perryton, Texas. It started in 2010 and ended in 2012-ish. Afterward, we went our separate ways. However, along our two-year adventures, so to speak, we found technology, perhaps junk, that was ahead of our time. As one might put it, artifacts from the future."

"Who exactly are 'we', Commander?" Admiral Amaya interrupted and asked of Brian.

"Randy, if you would," Brian said, forcing Randy to answer the question.

Randy looked to Amaya, and answered the question almost hesitantly, implying that he didn't want to answer it. "Gabe Romero, myself, Brian, Billy Fonder, and Josh Disinell. Terry Farran and Angela Jones were included, but were not one of us. The only reason Lauren and Meghan are here now is because Lauren is now a close friend of us all and Meghan is Gabe's ex-wife yet still close friend. For whatever reason they still have a friendship, I don't know, but here she is."

Brian heard enough to continue. "We used this technology to our advantage whenever it was called for and to engage in bratty, teenage juvenile behavior. Such technology included engines that exceeded incredible speeds, holographic emitters, cloaking devices, and computer systems. Now we are using this technology to save the lives of the future."

"Commander," Rustin asked of Brian, "am I correct to assume that it is your group's belief that you were meant to find this 'technology'? Perhaps we are speaking of some sort of predestined time paradox."

"To the best of my knowledge," Brian answered, "T5B does not believe in this predestined paradox you speak of."

As Rustin nodded, Amaya interrupted as well, "Forgive me, but science was not my strongpoint.

What is this predestined time paradox you speak of, Commander Rendetti?"

"Sir, a predestined time paradox is where..." Brian started but was interrupted once again by Gabe.

Gabe's tone of voice again showed spunk and resentment toward something that wasn't yet explained, "Save it, White Man," referring to Brian, "let an expert in the field explain. Meghan, enlighten them."

Meghan glanced at Amaya, awaiting approval.

"Before we continue, Miss Overbay, what are your credentials?" Amaya asked of her.

"I hold a Masters in Temporal Mechanics at Stanford and work as the Assistant Director of the Science Department at Oral Roberts University in Tulsa, Oklahoma. I continue to go on my free time towards a PhD in said field at California University of Technology. What can I say; I am a genius."

Obviously impressed, Amaya nodded, "Very well. Explain this predestined time paradox."

"First of all, sir, it is not called a predestined time paradox. There are several paradox names and theories, but the one we speak of is called a Predestined Paradox. For example, the theory states that one person's very existence is determined by a future action by oneself in the past. Suppose you, sir, are to go travel back into time sometime in your life and somehow end up impregnating your great-great grandmother, who in turn had your great-grandparent. The chain would continue to your great-grandparent to your grandparent to your parent that is offspring to them and so forth and then to you. In theory, your very existence in this hypothetical scenario states that you are a direct descendant of yourself."

"Very well, Ms. Overbay, your explanation is quite understood. Now if we may continue," Amaya continued uninterrupted, "This basically comes down to the point that your group, Commander Rendetti, are predestined to save, or not to save, the future of humanity by some future action of some individual because of your findings of these 'future artifacts'. And, in turn, this individual is also part of his or her own predestined paradox to leave the technology in the T5B's capable, or not so capable, hands, back many years ago. And if this person did not travel back into time to let you 'find' this technology, Earth would've been doomed, therefore, leaving T5B to live an ordinary life in their own respect. And by living a normal life outside of your normal adventures, so to speak, you never would've been chosen for this mission, and regardless of the outcome, whoever else might have been chosen, would have failed; that is, if we are to assume that you are going to be successful."

"You have the general idea correct, Admiral," Meghan stated.

Captain Porter spoke, "So, how did you acquire this technology?"

"That is classified information held under T5B General Order Three." Brian responded.

"What exactly is T5B General Order Three?" Porter returned.

"General Order Three is a secret, or an oath," Randy interrupted, "An oath taken to the grave."

"Listen here," Porter addressed them all, leaning back in her chair, "I do not care about any oath or secrets you may have with one another. Is there perhaps a prequel or sequel to this story that we are in or something?" She paused, obviously looking for a better explanation, "A book, a video, or something that might tell us how T5B came about?"

"Gabriel Rodriguez, in conjunction with Romeriscope Productions, previously released *The Adventures of the Five Brats: in Perryton, Volumes One* and *Two*." Brian responded, "They were a collection of short stories written in Gabriel's high school days, never to be published. They do tell how T5B came about, but there is nothing to explain how this technology was acquired. For all we know, it could've been a figment of Gabriel's imagination."

"So we will never know the history of T5B beyond this story and future ones?" Porter asked again, hoping to get a difference response.

"In the future," Randy intervened, "there may or may not be a prequel written to this series of books, which will eventually explain everything that is missing... and then some."

"So we will just have to wait and see, huh?" Porter asked him.

Josh interrupted the conversation, "Haven't you watched Star Trek, Star Wars, or the Dukes of Hazzard? They have their prequels, but you just have to wait for them."

Everyone stared at Josh blankly.

"I don't think that using fictional stories, movies or television series provides us with a good frame of reference," Porter said, annoyed.

Gabe stood up, as if he were a lecturer at a seminar, "Quite frankly, I don't care about any of this insightful conversation. The point of my interruptions is that we need to be getting to the freaking point. We all still don't know why we are here."

"Well, Mr. Impatient, we are about to get to that." Brian stated. "The real point is that we are going to Mars, so sit your happy ass down."

Scowling, Gabe complied with the order with hesitance.

"Now that we can proceed," Brian continued, "we are being sent on a mission to spend two years getting to Mars, setting up equipment and greenhouses, living there for a small amount of time, and then coming back, all in the hopes of it working."

"What Commander Rendetti is trying to say is that the real point of this mission is to determine if our life, especially agriculture, can sustain on Mars," Admiral Amaya stating, sitting straight up, hands on table, "so that by the time Earth's ozone dies, we are all off and sustaining our population there, thirty six million miles more away from the sun. Then we can fix Earth's ozone from afar and return to our planet that we have killed."

Lauren interrupted the Admiral, "Assuming everything is successful, Admiral, the real question I have is that if we can really repair or regenerate the atmosphere."

"Yes, Miss Stone," Amaya stated in return, "but in order to do it, we must all be off the planet to do it or whatever human is left on the planet will die. We can inoculate the animals and sea life, but we cannot do so for humans, or at least at present time we cannot and have not found an antidote, so to speak. By the time you return from Mars, we will know if we can survive outside of this planet."

"Okay," Gabe's loud voice interrupted again, "Assuming you all are accurate about this fun science-fiction fantasy you have going on here and the help T5B has given, who are we, in person and literally, to be the official Ambassadors of Earth on a potential deadly mission?"

"Have you been listening at all, Mr. Romero?" Rustin took this opportunity to provide his voice, "These time paradoxes, you and your group's contributions and each of you all's various knowledge are key factors in the success of this mission. We do not have many options here. We could either choose T5B or go out and find some ragtag team of oil drillers led by Bruce Willis and hope for the best."

"That is true," Gabe agreed, "the last thing we need is a sequel to that crap."

Amaya took another turn at speaking, "Commander Rendetti has vouched for each and every one of you."

Gabe spoke again in a deeper tone of voice, as if he were accusing Brian of something horrific and despicable, "You vouched for us?"

"Save it, Gabe." Brian seemed to be more annoyed now than when he had started. "You all have been chosen for this mission for your specific skills."

"Oh," Gabe said even more irritated, "and what would that be?"

"You were chosen because of your excellent leadership skills." Brian stated flatly.

"And I suppose me owning seven Sonic Drive In's has something to do with that?" Gabe said.

"Yes, it does, Gabe. Randy, you are good in the weapons department, yourself being a Sergeant for the Amarillo Police Department. Josh, you have excellent negotiating skills as per your profession, which we will not discuss at this moment. Terry, you are computer ha… uh, expert, and Billy, you have excellent mechanical abilities, considering your profession. Lauren and Meghan, we need sex appeal."

Both stood up, obviously offended at the remark.

"Relax, ladies," Brian said, waving a shrugging hand, "Meghan, we all already know why you are here. And Lauren, your geology background makes you a perfect candidate as well."

Again Gabe argued, "I must protest. We are ordinary people…"

"With extraordinary talents," Amaya finished for him. "The point is that what they say is that, and you all are going, like it or not. If you wish to protest, you can go to jail right after you come back from your mission. You can say that you are not needed, but in reality, everyone is, especially T5B. While we may know the technology,

T5B understands it. In two hours, you are to meet Captain Porter in the courtyard to this Navy yard to begin preparations and coordination for boarding the ship." He didn't let anyone interrupt him this time, as he was standing and everybody else was watching intently, as if they were a kindergarten class listening to their strict teacher. "And let me remind you that this conversation and what is said in this room is classified, and I am not kidding about prosecution for treason against the United States. And with that being said, this meeting is adjourned."

He gathered his papers and walked out, apparently not happy, according to his posture and the way he walked out the room. As everybody cleared out and made their way to their own destinations, Gabe's friends did the same. Randy glanced at Gabe, gave him a disappointed look, and left.

After everyone cleared out, Gabe and Brian were the only ones remaining.

"You vouched for us?" Gabe started.

"It only seemed wise." Brian countered.

"Why us, Brian?" Gabe declared, again trying to argue an almost undeclared point.

"We're not going to go through this again, Commander Romero."

"Commander?"

"We'll sort out the details later, Gabe. Get used to it."

"You know, I have a real bad feeling about the whole situation, Brian, and you are making it worse."

Brian grew sterner as the conversation continued, "Deal with it, Gabe. We are ordered to be a part of history and historic events, so now we, as a whole group, will get the famous, not infamous, status that we always wanted."

"There's no winning, is there?" Gabe asked again.

"No, there is not. For one, you don't even know me anymore, so grow the hell up. And for two, show some freaking respect for the military, who give their lives every day for this country and the security of the world. It'll all be over before you know it, and then you can contemplate your actions in prison for treason while someone else takes over your precious franchise." Brian shook his head, and before Gabe could interrupt again, he walked the other way.

Gabe stood there, alone, as Brian left the room.

CHAPTER 2

---THE USS FRONTIER---

"Welcome aboard the United States Starship *Frontier*." Captain Porter pronounced after the whooshing of the elevator doors revealed Gabe and his friends. Brian stood on the right side of Captain Porter.

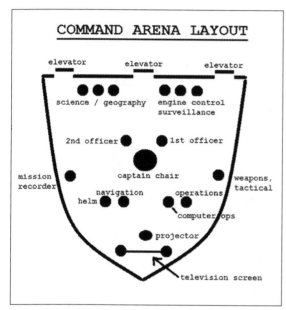

"This is the Command Arena," Porter explained. The starship *Frontier* was frequently referred to as a shuttle-plane, as the outside of the ship resembled a greatly oversized space shuttle. The rest of the ship was designed after an airplane. The wings were the classic example, which was where the engines and motors that made space travel were placed. The ceiling inside the Command Arena was placed at the nose of the ship and spanned three stories high. The ceiling inside the Command Arena curved to the contours of the ship, all the way down to eye and floor level. The lighting inside the entire ship had basic sconces along the walls a meter or so apart so that darkness never threatened. The middle of the ceiling had a bulbous light fixture that took the role of the main light of the Arena, as the smaller, lesser-watt floodlights took the role of not letting darkness threaten anywhere. The elevator was built in as it would be in an earthly skyscraper. It was hidden in the walls, reading to go to any of the higher or lower decks, but since this was the only elevator on board, it was set up in a grid-like pattern to go sideways to the other exits on each perspective deck.

The decks were letter named, A through F. Decks A and B were at the top, Deck C was at Command Arena floor level, which an opposite door in the elevator allowed access. Decks D through F were bottom decks. The higher decks were reserved for mission purposes, and respectively, the lower decks were dedicated towards quarters and accommodations. Each personnel officer aboard the ship had their own access code to allow limited access in accordance to each person's clearances.

"The Command Arena?" Gabe questioned, glancing around, not attempting to leave the elevator.

"Yes, Gabe, the Command Arena," Brian said with a sarcastic tone of voice. "What would your stupid series call it?" He waited for a response, but realized quickly that he wasn't going to get one. He finally explained himself, "You know, The Bridge..." he paused, waving to prompt an answer out of Gabe, "Star Trek?"

Gabe stared at Brian blankly for a moment, and then responded, with a slight annoyance to his voice, "Right."

"But we're a little more mature than that," Porter said, interrupting right away. "We prefer to use grown up terms here, and save the Navy standard term of 'bridge' to earthly vessels."

Gabe glanced at Randy and then stepped out of the elevator and came real close to Captain Porter, almost as if he was a drill sergeant to a trainee on the first day of boot camp. "So, Captain," Gabe said, their faces a mere inch or two apart, "Speaking of being grown up, how did a young lady like you get the Captain's Chair so quickly?"

"Expertise and ingenuity," Captain Porter responded, not flinching or backing away. She realized from Gabe's tone that this might be a battle of the wits.

"Is that right?" Gabe asked, almost too smugly. "Perhaps your superiors, such as Rustin and Amaya, got paid with more than just money."

The Command Arena, which was cluttering with noise from personnel and machinery, suddenly became very quiet...

...and without warning, a cricket chirped, as if everyone were on a field or prairie on Earth during the dead of night.

Instantly, Porter knew what Gabe was implying, and his anger to being recruited to the *Frontier* were feeding his comments. She knew she may be forced to arrest him if this pursued beyond her abilities to diffuse the situation. "Mr. Romero," she said with stern firmness, "I warn you once: watch your mouth."

"What's the matter, Captain? Are you afraid the truth is too well seen? What about Brian here? Is he teaching you to be a *smart ass* or are you just attempting to step out of that dirty blonde colored shell you got going on there?" He pointed to her hair in the process.

Porter ran out of patience, and snapped back, "No, Gabe, instead of being a *smart ass*, as you always seem to be, I strived to be a *wise ass*, and make a real career and a real job for myself instead of smelling like grease all the time. Now, what *dumb ass* would do something like that?"

Gabe's quick wits allowed for a quick comeback, "Well, apparently some *stupid ass* needs this grease trap for his leadership skills. Correct me if I'm wrong."

If she let him get away with talking to her like a demeaning supervisor to a subordinate trainee, how could she expect professionalism and proper chain-of-command respect from her crew?

"I have enough of my own, thank you very much, Mr. Romero. So, therefore, if you wish to continue, we can have this argument on opposite sides of the brig and you can contemplate the next *two friggin' years* why you chose to argue with a decorated Marine Captain."

Gabe was about to say something, but Porter placed her finger on Gabe's lips, stopping him as she continued, "Hush, because when you get back to Earth, you will also be arrested, charged and imprisoned for treason along with charges of insubordination."

Gabe, realizing that he might have taken things a bit too far, backed away and extended his hand out to shake Porter's hand, "My apologies, Captain."

Brian and everyone else sighed a heavy sigh of relief, knowing that Gabe finally conceded, and attempted to make peace for once.

Porter, on the other hand, had to make an example for those watching her, "Let me tell you something, Mr. Romero. The next time you speak to me in that fashion, you will be immediately arrested, no questions asked. I don't care if you are the ringleader of T5B or just some random extra that's placed along here in this story, right now or in the future. You will follow my orders just like everyone else on this ship, and you will show some respect to me as your Commanding Officer, whether you like it or not. Do I make myself clear?"

Gabe huffed, as if he was annoyed, "You can't accept an apology, can you?"

It was almost as everyone practiced taking breaths together, rehearsing for some choir concert of a sort. They could almost see Porter issuing an arrest order the very next instant.

"Do, I, make, myself, clear!" Porter asked one last time and as most firm as she could without yelling.

Resuming proper posture, Gabe affirmed, "Yes, Captain."

"Good, I knew you would see it my way," Porter said egotistically, almost as if she were a high school cheerleader winning an important argument against her rival nemesis. Turning around, she then commanded, "Marines."

An apparent pre-appointed group of Marines walked up to her and stood in a single formation, hands to their sides. "Captain," they all responded together.

"Lieutenant Mark Gonzalez will assist you, Mr. Pickings, in learning our weapons and their associated systems, consoles, techniques and procedures. After all, if we collide into an asteroid because you didn't know how to use the lasers and missiles properly, we'll all be dead," Porter ordered and explained. Randy nodded, as the Lieutenant did the same to confirm.

Porter continued uninterrupted, "Private Kelly Curtis will assist you, Lauren and Meghan at the science consoles, as well as teach you to read, understand and use them.

"Terry, Professor Charles Élan will help you understand how our computers systems and work and how they are set up as well as network information that you may need. Josh, Private Duke Zeron will help you understand how to act in front of the camera to negotiate or debate as per our procedures.

"Billy, go to the Engine Room on Deck C and report to Commander Rabbet Vahns. He will show you around the engines and operations center. Remember, all of you have two days to learn, so learn quickly. Proceed." Porter ordered one last time.

As per order and without question, they all took their turn leaving for their designation. Gabe, Porter, and Brian remained.

Raising an unsure hand, Gabe asked, "You forgot me, Captain."

"No I didn't; report to me in my office at 1700 hours in two days. In the meantime, feel free to settle in, get used to your surroundings and take a tour. In fact, Brian will give you the official tour and accompany you like a lost little puppy while on the ship until you are speed-trained and feel comfortable by yourself." Porter explained.

"You are kidding me, right?" Gabe responded quickly, not happy that he was stuck with his present-day arch nemesis.

"You will follow my orders, remember?" Porter stated very clearly and in a slower tone of voice.

"Yes, Captain," Gabe said without hesitation.

Brian smiled, apparently happy with the arrangement, and waved his hand in a gesture, "This way, please."

The whooshing of the elevator doors sounded as Gabe and Brian exited onto A Deck from the elevator. "This is Deck A," Brian said.

"Really? You've got to be kidding me?" Gabe said, overemphasizing his sarcasm.

Ignoring the comment, Brian continued, "Basically this and Deck B are reserved for mission purposes, so that means we can skip Deck B."

"Good."

"Pretty much whatever mission we go on, we work on that on A and B, unless we need the land rovers, which we use on the aft end of Deck F, which you will see shortly."

"Not if I can help it," Gabe said again with an irritated tone of voice.

They started to walk back to the elevator when Brian stopped at an entryway to a room of a sort, "All rooms and doors aboard *Frontier* have a hand print identification panel along with this keypad next to it to allow access to only authorized individuals. You have your own separate pass code that is changed weekly to prevent any unauthorized access in accordance to your security clearance."

"Uh huh," Gabe said, showing no interest.

Brian placed his hand on the handprint screen as a demonstration. After the screen scanned it with a white line, it blanked out and was replaced with a statement written in simple dot matrix-like font, "ENTER PASSCODE ON KEYPAD." Brian entered his pass code on the keypad with his other and the door opened, revealing a science lab of a sort with two unknown Marine officers working inside at a table lined with beakers. After acknowledging Brian's existence, they turned back to what they were doing prior to the interruption.

After five seconds, the doors shut, sensing no one was in the entryway or had entered the room.

Brian tried another tactic, "These pass codes and handprint identification monitors on each door can also be used to block someone when they decide to be a pain in the ass."

"Yup, that would be me." Gabe said, as that statement caught his interest. He then blew on his fingernails and polished them on his shirt.

Rolling his eyes, Brian led Gabe back into the elevator...

...and moments later, walked out with him on Deck C. Brian continued his tour, "Deck C is the center of operations for the entire ship. The more important rooms are located here, in the center of the ship, in a manner of speaking."

"Uh huh," Gabe said, back into his uninterested mode.

"Here you can also find Sickbay, so to speak."

"This isn't the *Enterprise*, jackass." Gabe said, as the Star Trek innuendo caught his attention.

"Okay, the term we use is the Infirmary. That is located on this deck, as well as the Flash Technology Room." As he sensed that Gabe was about to interrupt with a sarcastic remark again, he spoke before Gabe could do so, "You see, this platform we are on and see that to our left and right, they lead back to the other elevator doors. These steps here in front of us," he said, pointing to a set of steps, leading up to an upper level, "the upper floor is actually Deck C-1 and this lower one here is Deck C-2. Deck C-1 houses the Infirmary, Flash Technology Room, and places like that. Deck C-2, on the other hand, consists mostly of the Engine Arena, Missile Control and the Magnetic Gravity Generator Room."

"What's a magnetic gravity generator?" Gabe asked, showing real interest for the first time since being on the mission.

Brian explained casually, "The boots they gave you to wear on this ship are outfitted with special magnets, as well as the floors of the ship. They work together to keep your feet on the floor. Without them, you'd float around, and as you already know, you cannot take them off by order of the Marines, except for bed or shower."

"And what happens when we sleep?" Gabe asked.

"You'll find loose fitting seatbelts on your bed for that," Brian explained further."

"That sucks," Gabe said, "so what happens if we did take them off and the ship zooms through space? Won't we smoosh into the wall?"

"First of all, genius, the ship goes fast, but it doesn't go fast like a drag car. It takes time to get to the speeds we travel. And as for your question in that regard, the lower level houses the Inertia Control Room."

"Cool, I see." Gabe said. "Are we done with this crappy tour yet?" Gabe had lost interest once again.

"Wouldn't you like to learn about the newest technology we have: Flash Technology?" Brian asked.

"No, I could care less about it." Gabe countered immediately.

"But you might need to know this in the future," Brian informed him.

"Seriously, Brian," Gabe said, his tone turning into a more irritated one, "I don't really care about any of this technology that we supposedly offered to the military, and let's hope that we can get this done in the most quick and efficient possible manner. I don't care about any tour of a ship I will never be on again after this mission and in answer to you: I don't need to know any of this in the future. This isn't high school math class to hone your logic skills, Mr. Spock. Do you understand what I am saying?"

"Why do you have to be such a butt head about everything, Gabe?" Brian asked, almost pleading.

"Because I don't like you and I sure as hell don't like this predicament you put us in," Gabe responded, and then walked backward into the elevator. He spoke once more, "One more thing. We're done with this tour."

Brian ran to the door, "We're not done…" but he ran into the door as it whooshed shut before he even had the chance to enter, "yet." He finished to himself.

The door opened again, and Gabe was standing there, smiling in the most fake smile he could muster up at the moment. "I am." Before Brian could react again, he closed the door, once again shutting Brian out.

"So, Captain," Gabe said to Porter in her office two days later, "We all received our crash courses and are speed-trained the best we can be in the allotted time. Everyone I know seems to be familiar with this dandy technology of yours, but we have yet to see any of 'our' own, so to speak."

Her office was set up like an executive office. It seemed a little empty for she only kept the important books and binders on the shelves. Gabe sat across from her as if he were being interviewed for an important executive job at a business firm on Earth.

"You are wrong, Mr. Romero," Porter corrected, "Our engines are in fact modified and inspired by the engines used in your heyday. The holographic emitters you found were used in designing a sophisticated view screen that is linked to every camera inside and outside the ship."

"View screen?" Gabe questioned the term.

"Yes, view screen, Gabe," Porter explained, "As you noticed, we have a giant white wall on the nose of the Command Arena. That allows the holographic projectors that are installed on each end and on the ceiling to create a 3D representation of the images the cameras are feeding back to us. We are seeing a hologram, but also a real-time image, almost like a security office at your local shopping mall. But there is also that one giant television in front of it, which is a 92-inch TV. The holographic systems are only used for back up, should the TV give out by whatever circumstance. Need I explain more?"

"No, that's fine, Ma'am," Gabe said while leaning back in the chair. "But Captain, one thing puzzles me."

"And what would that be, Mr. Romero?"

"You say our technology inspired all this technology and it's everywhere, so to speak. Billy's helping in the Engine Arena and Terry's getting all your computer glitches out, and that's about it." He clasped his hands together, "So tell me, Captain, why are we here? And don't tell me it is because we are here to share the glory and it is our expertise in this equipment because if that was the case, you only need Billy and Terry."

Pushing back her chair to get up, Porter said, "Well, Gabe, the media is involved. We cannot just credit ourselves. Think of it as you finding the comet that is doomed to crash on Earth and wipe out the planet in five years. That comet becomes Romero's Comet or Comet Romero or some other bull like that."

"The point, Captain," Gabe said a little more pushier this time.

"The point, Gabe," Porter said as she walked around to Gabe's side of the desk and leaned on the corner, holding herself up with her hands, "is that the USS *Frontier* is the first real starship to go out into space, built with technology that was either yours or inspired by what you and your group found. Your 'artifacts' helped make this ship possible, and four more are being scheduled to be built, with the second on the finishing touches. The *Frontier* is the flagship of Earth and an icon to the human race in our struggle to survive and explore outside of this world. T5B's technology is now put to a real test, because until now, we have only been able to use it under simulation."

Leaning forward toward Porter, Gabe said, "So, if something goes wrong, we get the blame."

Pushing herself back up to walk back to her chair, Porter waved a shrugging hand, "Relax, Gabe. Why are you always so pessimistic? We hope it doesn't have to come to that."

Captain Porter's walkie-talkie, which was clipped to her belt, chirped, "Terry to Captain Porter."

Grabbing the walkie-talkie and placing it her mouth, she pushed the button and spoke, "Porter here. Report."

"We are receiving an incoming transmission from the White House. President Larry Fischer is online wanting to speak to you before we depart from the United Nations Space Station."

"Understood, Terry. Porter out." She turned off the walkie-talkie and with a sensitive toss, threw it onto the desk. It slid for a few inches before coming to a stop on some papers. As she did so, she spoke to Gabe, "Commander Romero, let me make this crystal clear. Regardless of how you feel about me, Brian, this ship or this mission, I ask that you cooperate in the spirit of humanity. And you better believe it, if you screw up history for me, they will never find your body."

Assuming she was joking, taking into account the dryness in her tone of voice, Gabe let out an uneasy smile, and spoke in a sarcastic tone, "Are you threatening me, Captain?"

Again with a straight face and dry tone, Porter explained, "Yes, it is, and remember it well. No one can hear screams in or from space. And remember, I am asking you with a most pleasant and professional tone here, please?"

"Well, Captain, since you put it that way, I will place my attitude aside for the time being. I am done being a butthead for now." Gabe said while straightening his jacket and tie.

Porter finally smiled, "See, I knew you had a sense of humor, hiding in that jackass exterior of yours. As you know, you have been assigned as Commander Romero, my first officer. Commander Rendetti, your evil arch-nemesis, is my second."

Gabe resisted the urge to roll his eyes at the mere mention of that name.

She headed to the door, and Gabe followed. Speaking on the way out, Porter summed up her conversation with Gabe, "This is where you all's crash course training ends the trial phase and gets put into action."

CHAPTER 3

--UNEXPECTED COMPANY--

Captain Porter and Gabe walked into the Command Arena from the elevator. Lauren and Meghan were at the right rear end at the science consoles. Terry was at the front at Computer Operations controlling ship functions. Brian and Josh were standing to the left of the raised Captain's Chair. Billy was on Deck C-2 with Commander Vahns in the Engine Arena and Randy was at the weapons console.

"Josh, take that chair over by the Mission Recorder and observe," Porter immediately ordered, pointing and walking forward toward her chair, all at the same time. "Brian and Gabe, take your chairs."

Slightly touching the chair with her left hand as she came around the right of it, she spoke again, "Lauren, put the President online."

"Aye, Captain," Lauren responded, "it will take a second for the transmission to pass through, but all ends are online."

"Understood," Porter said as she turned back to the giant TV in front of everybody, and straightened up, prepared to salute the President.

Moments later, the television came on, but flickered on and off, staticy, almost like reception from way back in the primitive television antenna days. The audio systems cracked and chirped, but nothing came of it. Both systems seemed to be on the brink of failure.

"Meghan, report," Porter said, immediately turning around to ascertain the situation and get answers.

"Our visuals and computers are having a hard time connecting," she responded as she was entering commands into the console, "we'll have to cut transmission to the visual systems and give full power to the audio systems only so that we can receive."

"Do it, and Lauren, send an encoded audio message telling him what has happened," Porter ordered almost the instant Meghan finished explaining the situation, and then turned back around, "This is the USS *Frontier*, Captain Kristina Porter in command to the President of the United States. Come in please." She formed her posture, as if she was saluting the President in person.

After a small hesitation, the audio bounced back to her, "Captain Porter, this is President Larry Fischer from the Kennedy Space Center. It is a pleasure to send you off on this historic mission."

"Mr. President, touché," Porter said, at the moment unsure on how to respond to that statement.

"Captain Porter, as much as I'd love to give the order to get underway, I must confess there has been a change of plans. I am in preparations to get onto a smaller shuttle to head to and dock with your ship. You should prepare the docking clamp on Deck E, Section 3 near the aft starboard quarter of your ship. As you know, that section is set up for that specific purpose in need of an emergency."

"Yes, I am aware of that large room's purpose, Mr. President, as I already know my ship," Porter answered, "But may I ask why you are coming onboard?"

Brian and Gabe glanced at each other uneasily while President Fischer responded, "You have always been direct, even to a C.O., Captain, and that is why I will answer your question. I have received intelligence that the ship may not be as ready as I was previously led to believe. I must personally make a final inspection, return to Earth, and then give the order to get underway at the Oval Office. You do know the order and the Command Arena will be simultaneously broadcasted split-screen style to all residents on Earth, right?"

After a deep breath, Porter responded, "Yes, Mr. President."

Sensing her hesitation, Fischer responded, "At ease, Captain. Is there something wrong?"

While she took a deep breath, Gabe had stood up and stepped forward, interrupting the conversation, "Sir, my name is Commander Gabe Romero, First Officer aboard *Frontier*. There is nothing wrong up here nor is there any objection to any chance you take to make sure this is a success. We were just caught off guard."

'*What the hell is he doing?*' Porter thought as she was taken aback, but didn't interrupt him as she stared at Gabe speaking uninterrupted, "As a gesture of goodwill, may I invite you and your party to a formal dinner as honored guests aboard the USS *Frontier?*"

It was Fischer's turn to pause for the moment, and at best guess, could only be contemplating Gabe's offer, "Commander Romero, quite frankly, you were not in a position to interrupt your commanding officer. However, I do accept your explanation for the situation at hand and I accept your invitation. Captain, prepare that docking clamp. We will talk shortly in a few hours when I get onboard."

Porter nodded, as if he told her face-to-face, "Understood, Mr. President. Porter out."

Terry turned around from his console, "All communications are cut off, Captain."

As Porter turned toward Gabe with a look as if she was going to reprimand him, Gabe turned away and walked to the center elevator, passing the now-standing Brian on the way out. "See, I saved the day.

I hope you're happy." Gabe said in a loud whisper, obviously intending on everyone to overhear.

Before anything could be said or anyone could react, Gabe disappeared into the elevator, closing the doors immediately. The last image anyone saw was him staring out the elevator, straightforward and in no particular direction, with a stern demeanor on his face.

On schedule and a few hours later, the smaller space shuttle-like craft approached the *Frontier*. Gabe and Randy were the last to walk down the corridor on Deck E, dressed in proper attire.

Adjusting his tie, Randy spoke to Gabe as they headed to the docking room where everyone was supposed to meet the President, "Dude, she was pissed after you walked out the way you did earlier on the C.A."

"Yeah, she tore me a new one in my quarters shortly after. Why do you think I was stuck there until now? She confined me there."

Randy smiled, "Your dumbass deserved it. As your best friend, I would recommend shutting your mouth before you get arrested."

Raising an eyebrow, Gabe let one corner of his mouth smile, "Sir, yes, sir."

Returning a glance, Randy smiled back as they walked into the room.

Everybody stood in a straight line across the back wall of this oversized room as if they were in formation at boot camp. About a third of the way into the room long-way to the other wall was a sturdy Plexiglas divider, splitting the room into two rooms. Between the Plexiglas and everyone lining the wall was a triple station, manned by Vahns and Billy. They were simultaneously entering commands and doing their own thing to their own input devices while talking amongst one another. Porter stood to their rear left as Brian stood formally next to her. She had her walkie-talkie in hand and had glanced at Gabe and Randy as they walked in. Randy took his place along the wall with the rest of the assigned members as Gabe took his place opposite Brian at Porter's side.

"Terry," Porter spoke into her walkie-talkie as Gabe approached her, "is President Fischer's ship ready to dock?"

"Yes, Captain, they are signaling that they are in position five hundred meters off our bow."

"Very well, Commander. Aft-thrusters ahead one-quarter, port and starboard at station-keeping."

"Aye, Captain. We're getting into position now. We will signal Vahns' console when we're in position."

Porter didn't bother to acknowledge, but rather turned off her walkie-talkie and clipped it back on her belt where it belonged.

Gabe stood there as moments of uneasy silence followed.

"Captain," Vahns said a few seconds later, "we're clamping now. Brace for impact."

The ship shuttered, causing everyone to stumble slightly. Everyone made it almost unnoticeable as they regained their balance and regained their original formation. "Beginning interlock procedure," Billy informed everybody as he inputted commands into his console.

Moments later, the back wall of the room that everybody was facing began to opened up, revealing a hidden docking square that was opened up to the small craft the President was aboard. Once the walls stopped moving to the side, the Joint Chiefs and other personnel worked their way out through the gravity-less environment. The Plexiglas acted as the seal between the gravity plated starship and those exiting out of the craft. Near the Plexiglas on the President's side were safety bars spaced out so that people could position themselves properly on the floor so when gravity returned, they didn't fall or hurt themselves.

A few minutes passed as each took their spot on their respective safety bar. As President Fischer was the last one to exit, he was the last one to take his spot, almost center of the Plexiglas barrier.

"Commander Vahns," Porter ordered, "Initialize Revopro and prepare to raise the wall."

"What is Revopro?" Billy whispered to Vahns.

As Vahns inputted his commands to restore gravity plating and close the walls the docking square, he whispered back to Billy, "Revopro is the basically what one might think it might imply. The process we just witnessed is going in reverse. The docking square closes first, and then the walls that hide it. Gravity is slowly returned to normal so that there are no sprained ankles in the process. Finally, as an added touch, the invisible barrier in front of us that kept us from getting our lungs sucked out will raise halfway up, taking a place inside the walls of the ship in the upper two decks."

Billy nodded an understanding nod as the wall began to rise. Once the Plexiglas stopped, President Fisher stepped forward, ducked underneath the marked bottom, as did his associates and personnel. Immediately, everyone facing him from Porter's crew saluted him.

"At ease," Fischer saluted back and ordered as he walked toward Porter and her posse. "Captain," Fischer acknowledged as he stopped in front of her.

"Mr. President, welcome aboard the *Frontier*. We are honored to meet you, sir." She gulped, unsure on where to continue. After a second or two, she made her decision, turning to her group, "Mr. President, may I introduce to you to my first officer, Commander

Gabe Romero and my second officer, Commander Brian Rendetti." She gestured with her hands, making sure he could tell who was who.

Fischer walked to them and glanced them over, as if he were inspecting merchandise. "And over here," Porter continued, "is Randy Pickings, Weapons Manager; Josh Disinell," she paused second, unsure what to call him, "my advisor." She couldn't tell them he was a mediator, should something go awry. "And over here are Privates Duke Zeron and Curtis, and the rest are essential personnel."

As each one was introduced, Fischer went to each one and glanced at them the same way he did Gabe and Brian. "Captain Porter," she said after turning and walking back to her, "My personal security officer, General Cue, and my advisor, Sir Shanaus. The rest are, as you so lightly put it, essential personnel."

General Cue and Sir Shanaus did as Fischer did. After they shook hands with each one, Cue returned to Gabe, "Commander Romero, am I correct?"

"Yes, sir," Gabe replied formally.

"At ease, Commander," Cue said in a smug tone of voice, "You don't have to be uncomfortable or afraid."

Gabe literally looked up at Cue, who stood six-six compared to Gabe's five-foot ten, "I am not afraid, General Cue, not even of you." He returned his glance back to its original position.

Captain Porter stiffened, but remained silent and at correct stance.

"Very well," Cue said, obviously impressed by Gabe's bravery. Stupidity is what Porter would have called it. Cue continued, "It would be, shall I say, impressive, to fight with you with such a fearless attitude like that, however, it would be unfortunate for you if we were on opposite sides."

Again, Gabe looked Cue eye-to-eye, "I'm not sure how to take that."

Shanaus stepped forward, "I suggest you take that as advice."

This time, Gabe did not hold restraint, showing he didn't want to be there, "Have you ever considered another job other than Advisor? If not, perhaps you should, because you give terrible advice."

As Shanaus reared back in insult, Porter stepped in and interrupted what was sure to explode into a frenzy, "Mr. President, perhaps you, General Cue, and Sir Shanaus would like to get this inspection underway."

Fischer nodded in confirmation.

"This way," she said, leading the way out the door. Randy followed up the rear, shaking his head at Gabe and mouthing the words 'zip it' while he did a zipping gesture to his mouth with his fingers.

As everybody made their exit, Gabe asked, "Billy, are we done here?"

"Yes, we are. Go somewhere else and smart off," Billy responded as he and Vahns exited as well.

"Whew," Josh breathed out heavily, "I thought you were fixing to fight."

"Ha ha ha, not today," Gabe said, smiling to reassure.

Privates Zeron and Curtis then left, leaving Gabe, Brian and Josh alone in the room.

"Don't worry, Gabe. I'm on your side." Josh said.

"As so am I," Brian added.

Gabe's smile turned to a frown, "Oh yeah, are you now?"

"Really Gabe, I am," Brian affirmed.

Gabe took a step toward Brian, but Josh got in between them, "Enough!" He burst out, "This is childish."

Gabe looked at Josh, and then back to Brian. He spoke slowly, "Brian, who's side were you on when you forced our arm?"

"Gabe…" Brian said, but Gabe didn't let him speak.

"No, Brian, this isn't about fame. This isn't about making history. And this is most definitely not about our past. This is about talking to people who are supposed to be your friends first before involving them in what could be the deadliest mission known to mankind."

Brian stood his ground, "Gabe, this conspiracy or deadliness you think is going on here is just in your head. There's no sign…"

Again, Gabe interrupted, "Sign smine! I don't look at signs, Brian. That's probably why I got so many traffic tickets. I have a real bad feeling about this and thanks to you, it's all coming true."

Brian studied Gabe for a moment, and was about to speak, but just as he took a breath to start, Gabe turned the other way and walked out of the oversized docking room.

Brian looked at Josh, hoping for support. Josh already knew that look from Brian, "He's right, Brian, regardless if he's being a dirt bag about it." Josh walked out the door, leaving Brian alone.

CHAPTER 4

----BATTLE STATIONS----

The door of the ship's mess hall opened. Gabe, Randy and Terry walked out. Walking briskly, Gabe straightened his tie, "Damn…" he stumbled, "that was one hell of a dinner."

Randy steadied Gabe, "Perhaps the drink of choice, Crown and Coke, was not a wise course of action."

"Save it, Randall Lou," Gabe snipped at him, "besides, the Crown took the sting out of recent events, thank you very much. And I'm fine, thank you," he stumbled again, but caught himself.

"Well, it doesn't look like they noticed," Terry said as Gabe looked at him.

"What do you mean?" Gabe asked.

Randy caught Gabe's stumble, again.

"What I mean," Terry explained, "is that even though you've had several drinks too many, it didn't appear that they noticed you are plastered off your ass."

"I ain't dru…" Gabe said, but fell in the middle of his sentence. As Randy helped Gabe back to his feet, Gabe held his stomach, "Oh, that's no good. I feel sick now."

"Randy, help him to his room. I'll meet you back on the Command Arena." Terry said calmly.

Randy nodded a confirmation as Gabe spoke, "Where'd the douche go?" He said, referring to Brian.

"Back to Summer's Eve?" Randy chuckled.

Terry, however, didn't smile, apparently not amused at the joke. He stood there, apparently waiting for them to become more serious. Randy spoke first, seeing that Terry was not thrilled at all, "Brian, or Mr. Douche as you put it, went with

Captain Porter and Privates Zeron and Curtis to escort the President back off the ship."

"Oh, okay," Gabe said, now somewhat serious. He noticed Terry started to walk away, "And Terry," he called out.

Terry turned around, "Yes, Gabe?"

Gabe pointed a drunk, unsteady and shaky finger, "We all had Crown, so I'm sure I ain't the only one that's wack."

"I know, but we can cover it up, unlike you," Terry smiled and then turned around to walk the other way.

A few minutes later, Randy and Gabe walked into Gabe's quarters.

"Well, Gabe, here you go," Randy said. Gabe sat onto his bed as Randy went into the cramped kitchen area. "About Brian," Randy started.

"Please don't," Gabe said quickly.

"This has gone too far, Gabe," Randy said again.

"And I said 'don't'," Gabe clenched his jaw.

Both were then silent for a moment as Randy started making himself a peanut butter sandwich.

"You know," Randy noted, "our quarters are awfully tiny."

"Yeah, think of it as an 'efficiency' efficiency apartment," Gabe responded, "everything's just shoved together in one big room."

"It kinda reminds me of a hotel room," Randy stated as he took a bite of his newly made sandwich. He took a moment to swallow the bite, "At least the restrooms get their own room. Otherwise, it'd be jail."

"Ha," Gabe said as he took off his military jacket, and then spoke softly, "Randy, you know I don't hate Brian."

"I know," Randy said.

"We tried to be friends, but agreed to be just associated after our little bitch spat, but it just didn't work out. What got me mad was that he turned us all into diplomats and Marines, something most of us in the group know nothing about. And worst of all, he did this all without our permission."

"Yeah, I know. I was pretty ticked also, but what can you do, you know? It is what it is." Randy agreed but continued, "What happened between you and Brian, if you don't mind me asking?"

"You don't know?" Gabe was a bit confused.

"I know Billy's contraption as well as Terry's version," Randy stated.

"Well," Gabe started his story, "Back when we had that bachelor party for Billy's wedding to Jennifer, I was just chillin' on the sofa, drinking a Coors Light…"

"You're name's Gabe?" a girl approached Gabe as he sat on the sofa at his Chris' house. Chris, Gabe's brother, always hosted the parties for the group back in their day.

"Uh, ya, it is, why?" Gabe had responded to the girl, who seemed like she was taller to him, but only because she was standing and he was sitting. If they had stood side by side, she would stand five inches shorter than he would.

"Because I know who you are," she said casually and sat next to him, drinking her own beer, "My name's Brooke Taylor."

"Brooke, huh," Gabe gave a confident nod, "are you here alone?"

Brooke paused a moment, as if trying to think, "Yes, I am. I barely know anybody here."

"Well, then," Gabe said, cracking a smile, "should I get you another drink." He gestured to her almost empty glass with his glass.

"Wait a second," Randy interrupted Gabe's recollection, "This story is too long to have a flashback, so cut to the chase."

Gabe chuckled, but briefed up the best he could, "I was under the impression she was with nobody, and I ended up stuffing her like a Thanksgiving turkey. The next morning Brian walks in and caught us. They had hooked up before the party and came in together, a fact I had never known. To make a long story short, I had got up and was in my boxers when Brian demanded to know what the hell I was doing. I still was trying to wake up and figure things out when Brian decked me and we got into the fight. Of course, Brian had the advantage cause of the cheap shot and had the better of me when Terry and Billy stormed in the room, breaking us up. The she had the nerve to say I was the one who got her drunk and porked her."

"What a bitch, dude," Randy said, almost laughing.

"What's so funny?" Gabe asked, almost irritated.

"Nothing, man," Randy said, clearing his throat, "It's just that you never defended yourself in the whole charade. One minute you and Brian are best buds and the next you are mortal enemies."

"Well, I did get her drinks and I did bang her, so I guess technically I did get her drunk, but I would've never even tried anything with her if I had known she was with someone, especially someone like Brian."

"So I presume you and Brian haven't spoken since you became rivals?"

"Yah," Gabe said, "The only reason I asked for Brian at the meeting was that the military asked that the original T5B gang be there, and Brian was the only one missing besides Angela, but we all knew why she couldn't make it."

"I see," Randy said.

Letting his jacket drop to the floor, Gabe said, "And this whole mission; I don't know."

"What do you mean?" Randy asked, intrigued.

"Look at everyone, especially General Cue. He shows off like he's some kind of hot shot jerk and walks around like he has a corncob stuck up his hiney hole, as if he's some super macho top gun."

"Well, he is a four star general, you know." Randy said.

"Well thank you for that information, Captain Obvious," Gabe said, "I didn't mean it on that level. Besides, they're all jerks, I guess… and kinda ugly." He chuckled at the last statement. Randy laughed.

"Uh HUM!" somebody coughed.

Instantly, Gabe and Randy stopped laughing and turned their attention to the door, the source of the cough.

A Caucasian female, very petite and about six inches shorter than Gabe, who was five-ten, stood at his open door.

"I am Lieutenant Stacey Norton. I work in the Command Arena with Terry." She said.

Gabe stood up, and spoke in serious demeanor, "You could've knocked."

She glanced at Randy and then back to Gabe. Randy was already up on his feet, standing. "Sorry, sir. I just wanted to meet you face-to-face myself."

Gabe looked at Randy, and then turned back around, "Lieutenant, can we talk about this some other time. I'm really tired."

"Yeah, I'm gone. I have to meet Terry. I'll see you in the morning, Gabe," Randy interrupted, shoving the last bit of his peanut butter sandwich in his mouth while speaking. He made his way to the door.

"Hasta pasta," Gabe said.

"See you later, man," And with Randy's final say, he disappeared out of Gabe's quarters.

Gabe turned back to Stacey, and spoke in an almost rude tone of voice, "Can I help you?"

"May I speak freely, sir?" She asked.

"I am not your superior, Lieutenant."

"Technically, you are, sir, and call me Stacey."

"Okay, Stacey," Gabe said, pausing to sit back onto the bed, rubbing his eyes, "Go ahead."

"It is an honor to work with you, sir."

Gabe looked up, "What?"

"I said, 'it is an honor...'" she started but Gabe interrupted.

"Yah, I heard you, but why?" Gabe said, shaking his head.

"You, Randy, Brian and the others have shown us the full potential of your technology. And plus if you don't mind," she sat down next to Gabe, leaving no space between them, "if I may say so myself, you are cute, sir, very," she said, pausing as she closed the distance between their lips, "very, cute." She didn't give Gabe time to respond and kissed him.

After a few seconds of slow, intimate kissing, Gabe pushed on her shoulder slightly, breaking the kiss, "If circumstances were different," he said while reopening his eyes, "I would be flattered. Some other time, perhaps."

After barely touching her lips to his again, she responded in a disappointed voice, "Of course, sir." She then slid her hand up his leg from his knee.

Gabe immediately proceeded to help her to the door, pulling her by the arm, "And Stacey?"

She turned around at the doorway, "Yes, sir?"

"Call me Gabe," Gabe returned the smile.

She smiled again and then left. Gabe shut the door and collapsed onto the bed, closing his eyes while he took a deep breath.

As soon as he planted himself on the bed, his walkie-talkie buzzed, "Captain Porter to Gabe."

Gabe opened his eyes, and used his right hand to fish for the walkie-talkie, which was on the nightstand by his bed. Once he retrieved and steadied the walkie-talkie to talk, he spoke into it, sounding perturbed, "What?"

"Meet me in the Command Arena, Commander."

He sat up and picked up his jacket.

"And Gabe," Porter continued over the walkie-talkie.

"Yes…" Gabe said, even more demanding than last time.

"We have our own dedicated channel on Earth and I am sure they are watching, so behave."

"Aye, aye, Captain," he said mockingly and made his way to his door, clipping his walkie-talkie to his side. Looking both ways as if he were crossing a street, he noticed Stacey going into the elevator. "Stacey!" He yelled out.

She looked up from her center position in the elevator.

"Hold that door!" Gabe yelled out loud as she held the door open for him. Quickly, he ran in. He felt tense and uncomfortable standing next to her after what just happened.

Gabe stepped out of the elevator doors. Terry and Porter were there to meet him. "Gabe," Terry said, "our computers are reading gases all around us." Everybody stared at him and Stacey, who seemed a little embarrassed. Gabe had walked out with his shirt un-tucked and tie halfway done.

"Terry," Gabe said, not realizing what was implied at their entrance onto the Command Arena. "We're all bound to have gas sometime, and besides, this really isn't a good time."

"Gabe," Porter interrupted, "Look at these readings." She pointed to Meghan's display as Meghan inched away to let them study the monitor. Porter continued, "This is showing that we are leaking a lot of fuel, or gas, as Terry put it, into space."

Straightening and tightening his tie while studying the monitor, Gabe turned his attention to Lauren, who was sitting a few feet away at her station, "Lauren, don't we have some kind of sensors to tell us why and to pinpoint the exact leak location?"

"Well, yes, but we don't have a camera on the underside of the ship. We only have this tactical diagram. The only notation my station is giving me is that it's coming from the interior engines, three and four." She jerked her head slightly to the giant television display in the front of the Command Arena.

Everyone's attention turned to the screen. On it was a basic 2D diagram representation of the *Frontier*'s underside with blinking squiggly lines representing gas leaks coming out from underneath the engines.

Gabe turned to another person, "Randy, do you detect anything unusual from your station?"

"Other than you walking out here with your clothes halfway done and Stacey next to you, no," Randy responded, stating what everybody else dared not to.

"Josh," Gabe said, frowning at Randy's remark, "Does that monitor say anything unusual?" He pointed to the small monitor attached to the Captain's chair. Josh had planted himself on the first officer's chair, which was the closest chair to it.

Josh was holding his head as if he had a massive headache, but leaned forward to swivel the monitor and glance at it, "No," he said, pausing a second before continuing, "but everything right now is a little fuzzy."

Gabe smiled, knowing what he meant, "Hmmm," he said slowly, "then it's probably nothing. We'll just have to re-dock at the space station and get that fixed before we can continue."

Whoosh!

The ship vibrated and rumbled, causing a moment of silence as everyone wondered where it came from.

"Lauren," Captain Porter ordered after regaining her composure, "Report."

"Sensors and cameras are picking up a missile coming out of our ship off the forward bow launcher," Lauren responding, reading the results off her station monitor.

"Put it on the viewer," Porter ordered as she made her way to sit down in her chair.

The television flicked on the instant a missile had collided with President Fischer's smaller craft. The explosion caused the engine to separate from the craft and deviate away in the opposite direction. The smaller spacecraft slowly started tumbling toward Earth. The broken-off engine and the part where it separated from the craft were popping and sparking with light from the fires the missile caused.

"What the hell just happened?" Porter ordered to no one in particular. Everyone, up until this moment, had been staring in awe at the screen and frozen in place, as if they were watching a spectacular fireworks display. But as soon as Porter spoke, the Command Arena buzzed to life.

"Captain," Randy said as he read from his weapons station, "We just fired upon President Fischer's ship."

"That's impossible!" Terry exclaimed from his station, "I had all computers locked and secured."

"To hell if I know! I didn't do it!" Randy proclaimed.

Whoosh!

One more distinct vibration reverberated throughout the entire ship. Everyone turned to the screen again, only to see yet another missile head toward the slowly-spinning craft. This one hit the second engine, and created the same effect as the last time. The craft began a faster descent toward Earth.

Captain Porter spun toward Stacey, who was at a Command Arena Engine Control station, "Lieutenant Norton, take your station." She ordered, pointing to the Operations Station next to Terry's Computer Operations. "Terry," she said, who had been near Lauren's station during the first part of Gabe's entrance, "man your post and find out who fired those missiles. Lauren, open transmissions to that ship. Josh, get down to the Missile Control Room."

She punched a few commands into the arm of her chair, and within a second, Commander Vahns appeared on her small swivel monitor. She pulled to face her, "Commander, send Billy to Missile Control."

"Aye, Captain," Vahns said on their direct link, and then the screen went black, signifying he shut off his end of the connection.

Everybody went where they were told. Gabe, at this time, had finished straightening his jacket and tie and went to Randy's station. The events had quickly sobered him up.

"Where is Missile Control?" Josh asked at the elevator door.

Before Porter could counter a response, Stacey stood up and walked toward him, "I'll show Josh."

Porter nodded, too preoccupied at the sudden chain of events to realize that she told Norton otherwise.

"Captain," Meghan called out, "They are suffering from multiple breaches on their aft hull. Atmospheric pressure is slowly decreasing and implosion may be imminent."

"And they aren't responding to any transmissions," Lauren added.

"Missile Control," Terry called into his walkie-talkie, "Do you read?"

With everyone running around and things hectic all around, Gabe was unsure on what to do.

The inside of the craft consisted of three levels: one engineering level, one level dedicated for barracks and medicine, and one command level. Each were the size of the Command Arena aboard the *Frontier* but only one story high and layered one on top of the other with a single gate-like elevator with a control panel on the back end.

Fischer and two other men were in the barracks level as the gravity went out on the entire craft. They were at relative rest, standing while holding onto a separate bunk frame each. Their lights were flickering off and on at a slow, steady pace.

A male computer generated voice came on, "Warning! Elevators inoperative. Hull breach in aft storage compartments."

"We need to contact Cue," The President ordered his men, "Use that emergency ceiling panel to the Command Deck. He should be in there."

Spring boarding himself off the bunk frame, one of the men slowly made his way to the ceiling tile, and it was at that instant a camera flash flickered. It was only noticed as it happened when the lights dimmed out. Everyone turned to the direction of the flash, which came from the broken elevator gates in the rear of the deck.

One person, dressed in a spacesuit, appeared before them. The solar darkening lens on the helmet had been activated, as if to obscure the identity of him or her. He, or she, had a raised arm, aiming a handgun.

As the one remaining man holding his bunk rail headed to protect Fischer, Fischer ordered, "Get to that ceiling panel and find Cue."

As the first man headed to the ceiling panel, the unknown spaceman shot the gun, shooting him in the back. Blood oozed from him as the gun went toward the second man, who was still intent on protecting Fischer, firing once more. This time, it caught the man on the inner thigh area. As he floated in agony cradling his thigh wound, the gun turned a final time.

As the trigger was being pulled, the masked spaceman turned off the tint, revealing to only the President who he, or she, was. The bullet pierced Fischer's sternum, sending him backward in the gravity-less environment. As he went backward in agony, a flash of light flickered again, and the assailant was gone.

"Captain, we're receiving video and audio transmission." Lauren said to Captain Porter.

"Well, I'm glad we got that video fixed," Porter said as she turned to the screen. An instant later, General Cue was on the Command Level of the craft.

"Captain Porter, you are a traitor and have deceived us," he accused.

Captain Porter was stunned silent. Then suddenly it occurred to her: Earth was still online and they were watching everything unfold.

Gabe stood up from his chair and stepped forward, "General, we haven't fired," He insisted.

"You lie again, Romero," Cue snapped, "And for that you shall see what 'unfortunate' means for you. This is courtesy of us, the great United States." The screen turned black and showed a 'No

Usable Signal' label, indicating General Cue cut the transmission.

"Meghan, I want cameras on that ship." Porter ordered, and instantly, the screen came back on, showing the craft regaining control of itself with some kind of emergency thrusters and turned back around toward the *Frontier.*

"Gabe," Randy interrupted, "We did fire, or at least that's what our computers are saying."

"Gabe," Lauren added, "They have regained control and have locked warheads on us."

Gabe was speechless. He turned to the Captain for an answer.

"Defenses up, Red Alert," she ordered, giving Gabe his answer. A moment later sirens blared and the red alert lights came on. When under Red Alert, every other sconce dimmed off and five powerful strobes, which were placed ten feet up and across the back wall of the Command Arena, blinked on and off. The only similarities to the red alert strobes were common fire alarms found in any building or warehouse on Earth.

"Captain," Brian intervened, "opening fire upon the President's ship will not help us. For one, we don't know the status of the President. And for two, they are, by far, more well-equipped in weaponry and technology than we are. That's why the President rides only in that craft when in outer space."

"Shut up, Commander. It appears we have no choice." Porter ordered.

She hit a button on her chair arm, "Missile Control Room?"

"Billy here," Billy said, appearing on her monitor, "but Josh and Norton haven't arrived."

The Captain glanced around the Command Arena, almost desperately, "Zeron, Curtis, find them!" She ordered harshly.

"Aye, Captain," they both said simultaneously and headed for the elevator.

"Randy, bring up the weapons systems," Porter ordered again.

"Aye, Captain." Knowing what kind of mood she was in, Randy was not about to question her.

"Meghan, status," Porter swung around in her chair.

"They have regained control, and getting ready to…" Meghan called out as consoles exploded near her, rocking the ship.

"Weapons at your command, Captain," Randy called out from the other direction.

"Randy," Porter ordered as she swung around again quickly, "lock Atomic Missile Alpha One on their ship."

Gabe looked at Porter from his chair, shocked, "An atomic bomb?"

"Yes, Gabe. One lucky shot and they're over with," Porter said, and then turned to Randy again.

"Alpha One locked on and ready to fire, Captain," Randy responded before she could even speak again.

Porter pointed her finger, a mere second from giving the order, but Gabe stepped in her view, facing Randy, "Belay her order." Gabe ordered.

Porter pushed herself up quickly, shocked at the events that just unfolded. Everyone on the Command Arena had shocked looks on their faces, also surprised that Gabe had dared make such a move. Gabe had made bold moves in the past, but nothing this daring. "Gabe, *don't*." Porter commanded very harshly.

Gabe turned around to face Porter, "Brian's right. Don't open fire."

The port side elevator exploded, knocking the doors off their rollers and sent out a fireball that winced out a second later. The elevators were designed to be airtight, but in the heat of battle, the immense pressure surrounding the elevator shafts caused it to pressurize and explode. The ship lurched forward, knocking everybody to the floor. A split second later, everybody was back on their feet, as if nothing had happened.

"Captain," Lauren yelled out, "we are experiencing major damage to the starboard engines. Minor breaches."

"Randy, fire Alpha One, NOW!"

"NO!" Gabe yelled, but it was too late. Randy had hit the button on his console.

A moment later, everything shut down all the lights everywhere turned off. Deep whining sounds signified the computers dying out, showing that they lost all power.

"Some ship," Gabe's voice called out over the darkness, "one hit and we're through. Braaah-vo."

"Whoooopsies!" Randy's voice called out next in the pitch black Command Arena. "That was the power button instead. My bad." It was apparent that he had pressed the button again, as everything and all lights came back on, including the Red Alert Status.

Gabe spoke before anyone else had a chance, "Belay her order, Randy. Meghan, signal our surrender."

No one moved.

"Magnetic hull shielding at thirty-five percent," Terry called out.

"Belay that!" Porter said. She then looked at Gabe, shaking her head, her voice almost shaky, "Don't you dare!"

Gabe finally used his only weapon. "They're loyal to me, not you," Gabe snapped back. He took only a second to speak, but not turn his head, "Now, Meghan."

A moment later, Meghan spoke, "Cue has agreed and has ceased fire. He is also requested us to turn off our magnetic polarity shield so they can board."

Porter fumed. How could she let this happen? It was her ship! How?

"Send a message. I'm taking an escape pod to their ship, unarmed." Gabe said.

Brian stepped forward, "Gabe, let me go. I got you into this mess. Let me go."

"Oh, you bet your ass you're going. You did get me into this, so now's your chance to redeem yourself, Commander Cupcake," Gabe turned to Randy, "Confine Porter to her room. Terry, lock computers and get some new codes for them."

"They have agreed," Lauren interrupted.

"Also, Randy," Gabe said.

"What, Gabe?" Randy asked as he took Porter by the crook of her arm.

"Find Josh and Stacey," Gabe said calmly.

"I will," Randy affirmed.

Gabe walked to the starboard elevator and entered codes into the elevator console, summoning up the emergency elevator.

"Gabe, take this: for good luck." Meghan's voice said from right behind him.

He turned around to realize that Meghan was mere inches from him, holding up something in her hand. He studied it for a moment and then looked at Meghan, "That's my wedding band."

"Former wedding band," Meghan corrected, "Remember, we divorced some time ago."

Eye to eye, Gabe recalled, smiling, "Right."

"Gabe, take it," Terry said from across the Command Arena.

Instantly, Gabe turned to Terry, perplexed, "What?"

"T5B Code 52," Terry said, offering no explanation.

Gabe thought for a moment, and then nodding, as if remembering something important, "Oh right... Meghan?"

"Yes." She responded.

"According to Terry, I have to make this moment sappy. I'm not going to do just because he tells me to. I'll do it because I want to." Gabe explained, and paused, "I love you, Meghan. I always will."

She raised her hands and held his face, "I know, as do I." She said softly as she gave him a tiny, soft kiss, a single tear streaming down her cheek.

For no apparent reason, Randy smiled, perhaps for the sake of the moment.

Turning serious, Gabe put the ring on, and turned to Brian, "Let's go," he said as the elevator door opened, and Brian following, carrying a first aid kit. Before the doors shut, Gabe called out, "Terry keep things together till I get back."

"I always do," Terry smugly replied.

CHAPTER 5

---WHAT WILL HAPPEN---

The docking square opened between the President's craft and the emergency escape pod of the *Frontier* after they jointly connected. Unlike before, the process of docking was not necessary as they were designed for emergency use. Both ships disabled the gravity magnets upon docking and docked normally. Gabe and Brian pulled themselves out onto the Command Arena level of the craft. As soon as the docking square closed back up and the seal was ensured and everyone was on the floor, gravity magnets enabled, allowing normal walking maneuvers. They were met by armed Marines assigned to the President, who were wearing magnetic boots, standing on the floor and holding guns to Brian and Gabe's faces.

"You two are under arrest," one Marine informed them.

"Save it for later," Brian snipped, "we're here to help." He lifted his first-aid kit.

The Marines glanced at one another, "This way."

They led them to a floor panel that was already opened up near the elevator. From it was an unrolled fabric ladder made of heavy duty military grade material. It was rolled out down to the second level of the ship. Gabe and Brian looked to the Marines for instruction.

"Get down there and help him," the Marine ordered. He nudged them with his rifle-type gun.

They immediately climbed down to the second level. There in the middle of the room was President Fischer, lying on the floor with General Cue by his side.

When he saw Brian and Gabe walk toward them, he stood up, as if he were getting ready to fight. "Why have you deceived us?" he exclaimed.

As Brian and Gabe stopped in front of Cue and the Marines, Brian stopped as Gabe stood face to face with Cue, "I have deceived no one." Gabe said almost instantly.

"Do you have a doctor?" Brian asked, looking at the two.

"Yes," Cue said, "he's lying over there." He pointed to the body at the fellow who was shot in the back.

"Then let me help," Brian said, holding up his makeshift doctor's bag.

Cue nodded at the guards, who had their rifles nudged into Brian and Gabe's backs. As the guards lowered their guns, Brian knelt down and checked for a pulse. He found none, and started CPR, hoping it would help, but after a few times, he didn't get a response. As he stopped, he looked up at Gabe, "He's dead, Gabe."

"What happened?" Gabe asked Cue, still face to face with him like two boxing champs squaring off face to face on a promotional poster advertisement.

"One person flashed over here and killed him; that's what happened," Cue said sharply.

"Flashed?" Gabe asked, backing away, giving the obvious impression he didn't know what the terminology meant.

"You're a Commander and don't know our own technology?" Cue asked quickly and suspiciously.

In what seemed like the most ironic moment in his life, Gabe cursed in his mind, realizing that he *should've* listened to Brian earlier on the tour. Instead he had chosen to be a jerk about the whole situation at that point in time.

Although he had quick wits and could come up with an answer immediately, Brian answered for him, intervening, "It's a new technology that we've been testing and working on, so not everyone in the military is aware of the technology or how to use it, especially Gabe and the gang, who have only had two days to prepare for this. Anyway, it can instantly transport you from one place to another. All you see is a flash of light, sort of like a camera flash."

Cue straightened his tunic, having thought only for a mere second or two, "Unfortunate," he said, still facing Gabe. "Arrest them," he ordered, obviously to the guards but didn't turn away from Gabe. The guards pulled out their cuffs from their police-type belt encasing and grabbed Brian and Gabe's respective arms, cuffing their wrists.

The guards started to drag them away, but Gabe made it difficult, as if he were trying to get to General Cue, "You bastard." Gabe spat.

Meanwhile, aboard the *Frontier*, Terry and the crew had been listening over a tapped communications channel.

"Terry," Meghan said, "As you could tell, we couldn't make out the most of it, but only enough to say that they have been arrested."

Terry stared at her for a second, "Crap," He said and then continued, "I hereby assume command of this vessel as of now. If there are any objections, let me know and it would be noted."

No one spoke, obviously at a loss at what transpired and didn't know what to do. Their leader, Captain Porter, had been confined to her quarters and by technicality, Terry was officially the next person still onboard in the chain of command to take over the ship, and they knew it.

"Very well," Terry continued again, "Lauren, contact Admiral Amaya on Earth for instruction."

"Terry," Meghan interrupted, "we're receiving transmission from the President's vessel. Audio only."

"Let's hear it," Terry immediately said.

"To the commander of the *Frontier*. Gabe Romero and Brian Rendetti are being taken to Earth to stand trial. We order you to stay within 50 kilometers of the United Nations Space Station. Any other distance will be considered an act of war upon the United States." It was Cue's voice, and he stopped, apparently awaiting a response.

Taking a deep breath, Terry spoke, sitting down in a captain's stance and setting his arms firmly on the command chair's arm, "This is Lt. Commander Terry Farran of the *Frontier*. I am now in charge."

"Commander Farran, what happened to Captain Porter?"

'So much for idle chit chat', Terry thought, "She, uh," he started, taking a second to think, "Died during your attack."

Almost instantly, Cue countered, "Very well, Commander. Do you understand our request?"

"Yes, I do, but I am under the command of Admiral Amaya. We will comply until we receive instruction from him. I'm sure he will work something out."

There was a short pause, and then, "Very well, but make no attempt to move until then. If you receive any communique from Admiral Amaya, relay it to me."

"Okay, Terry out." Terry spun around to face Meghan and nodded for her to cut transmission. She looked back up from her console, winking to confirm that she had done so.

Terry grabbed the walkie-talkie from the command chair and pressed the button. "Randy Pickings, report."

"Porter's locked in her quarters and we found Josh and Stacey. They were knocked out on Deck C-1." Randy voice informed him moments later.

"Are they okay?" Terry immediately questioned.

"Yeah, dude. They're being examined in the, uh," Randy paused.

"The uh what, Randy?" Terry questioned.

"E.R., I suppose," Randy said again, trying to think of a synonym for what he was trying to name.

"The E.R.?" Terry asked, unsure of what Randy was trying to say.

"Well, what do you want me to call it: the hospital?" Randy's voice snapped back quickly.

Terry smiled, pausing for just a moment, "I see. Do you have information on what happened?"

"I really don't have much. Josh says he was walking in front of Stacey when he was hit and blacked. Stacey said she was walking behind and blacked first." Randy informed him.

"I see, Terry out," Terry said, tossing his walkie-talkie onto the captain's chair and then turned to Meghan and Lauren, walked up to them, and whispered to them as he approached the duo, "Meghan, Lauren, we need to piece together what happened her tonight. Lauren, please monitor all outgoing and incoming transmissions of any kind, and keep that presidential convoy in your sight."

"Okay," she replied formally.

"Lauren," he whispered again, turning to her, "there has to be someone on board involved, perhaps two or more, so don't exclude anyone in your investigation, even our friends. And don't forget about Josh and Stacey. Monitor all ship communications to earth, ours and theirs."

"Sir, yes, sir," Lauren sarcastically replied and turned back to her monitor.

As Terry started to turn the other way, Meghan interrupted, "Commander, Admiral Amaya sent us a message to return and head toward United Nations Space Station to rendezvous with another convoy from Earth and be boarded by superior personnel so that they can take over the ship from us."

Turning back around, Terry thought for a moment. He then said, "Forward the message to Cue. Lauren," he said while glancing down to her monitor, "I see that our communications ability has been lost, so we cannot confirm nor deny we got the message."

"But there's nothing wrong with…" Lauren said, but Terry interrupted her by reaching over and punching a series of commands into her touch-screen monitor screen.

"There," he said, without explanation, "now there's something wrong with them."

Looking perplexed, Lauren started but interrupted by Terry, "But…"

When she started, Terry pulled her head forward and whispered into her ear, "if we go hand over this oversized piece of junk they call a spaceship, we won't ever get Gabe and Brian out of there." He let her go and she nodded to confirm.

She went back to work as Meghan whispered to her as well, "Remember, Earth saw everything, from us firing to Gabe's snappy remarks. They will honor Cue's attempt to prosecute them."

From an office suite inside the Pentagon, Amaya was talking to General Cue via camera connections from his computer on the desk. "General Cue," he stated, "release the prisoners. There has to be some sort of misunderstanding with this situation and we must investigate further before we can make any definite arrests."

"The *Frontier* fired upon us, and there is no doubt," Cue said over the monitor. "There were obviously no other ships in the vicinity, so it has to be them. Someone then assassinated the president. Farran is already taken command of the *Frontier* out of protocol, so it leads us to suspect a mutiny. So they will stand trial when we land and transport them to the federal courthouse in D.C."

"The *Frontier* is scheduled to dock with the United Nations Space Station by 0900 hours," Amaya informed him.

"Yes, we know," Cue instantly replied, "they forwarded your message. From then on, they have been under communications blackout, refusing all transmissions with us. That leads us to believe even more in the mutiny."

"Well, are they there?" Amaya questioned Cue.

"Yes, they are," Cue explained, "I ordered them to stay."

Amaya squinted a tiny bit, in deep thought, wondering why the *Frontier* listened. Surely they would have done or said something, he thought, "Very well, General Cue. We will also see you within a few hours."

"Admiral, we're not releasing them. We have an armed escort on standby at Kennedy Space Center. And lest not forget, I outrank you. Any attempt to do otherwise would be considered insubordination and treason, charges you cannot afford to obtain on yourself."

"Very well, sir," Amaya agreed, "We will work things out when you get here. Amaya out." Amaya aimed his remote to the big screen on his wall and disconnected the connection.

Admiral Casey Rustin, who had been sitting in on the meeting, reached down and opened his leather briefcase bag, and pulled out a tablet. He powered it on, tapped a series of commands into it, and handed it over to Amaya. While doing this, he spoke to Amaya. "Sir," he explained as a tactical display of a sort lit up the screen, "this is what we have come up with. If we use the T5B cloak in a drone or on the ground Humvee, we have the manpower to take them out and get them to safety."

Reviewing the plan, Amaya responded after pondering for several moments, "Casey, as much as I believe and feel that these men are innocent, there's nothing much we can do about this. First of all, Cue has seniority and you heard him about insubordination and treason. Secondly, we have to follow the law here anyway, even without Cue's interference."

"Sir, we can make it look like an accident on the part of Cue, not us," Rustin argued.

"Casey, no," he said politely, "I want to save these men as well, but my hands are tied. Unfortunately, even if they are innocent, someone has to take the blame, considering everyone on this mission and the mission itself is the target of media attention of the world." He handed the tablet back to Rustin and leaned back into his chair, taking a deep breath, tired and unsure on where to proceed under the present circumstances.

"Terry," Lauren called out on board the *Frontier*, "The convoy Amaya sent us is requesting transmissions."

Terry pushed his command monitor aside and stood up from the command chair, "Put them on, audio only."

"I want Captain Porter,' a stern voice ordered immediately.

"She's not in right now," Terry started walking forward as he spoke, "but if you leave your name and number..."

"Enough, commander of the *Frontier*," the voice said, "This is Marine Captain Darrin Johnston. This is no time for jokes. Identify yourself and tell me where she is and why is your viewer offline?"

"Captain," Terry said seriously this time, "this is Lt. Commander Terry Farran. First of all, Porter is in custody at the moment and secondly, we have suffered considerable damage in the attack earlier."

"Commander, lower the defenses and prepare for docking procedures."

"Admiral," Terry was feigning frustration, "Gabe told everyone at the meeting on Earth in the first place. We would not operate this ship any better than you can. It seems that we have yet to figure that out. We've only been here almost three days. We can't learn everything."

"Then how in the hell did you raise your defenses when you got into the fight?" Johnston asked quickly and forcefully.

"That was Lt. Norton's job, thank you very much." Terry was more forceful this time.

"Fine," Johnston was apparently getting angry as well. "We're going to perform a special anti-magnetism flash aboard sequence then."

"Captain, what the hell is a special anti-magnetism flash aboard sequence?" Terry asked, never hearing of such a maneuver.

Johnston, on the other hand, lost his temper. At least to him, they were stupid schoolchildren who don't know any better and should have never been allowed on any kind of equipment of this magnitude. But from T5B's point of view, it's not like they were expecting to be enlisted in this sort of adventure, and more or less expected to know everything, especially when it comes to government military functions and jargon. Their continued sarcasm in the heat of seriousness was not helping their case either. "You fool. Ask Commander Vahns. He'll tell you the procedure. We will maneuver into position while you ask him, he briefs you and you set up the right procedures."

"Very well, Terry out." Terry said quickly, sat down and swung his captain's monitor toward him. "Terry to Commander Vahns, come in please."

After a few moments, Vahns' receiving end blinked into existence on the monitor, "Commander Vahns here, sir."

"What is a special anti-magnetism flash sequence?"

"You were never told, sir?"

"Apparently not, Captain Obvious," Terry said dryly.

Ignoring the dry humor, Vahns started his explanation, "Commander, anti-magnetism flash procedure involves a special scientifically created magnetic polarity field onto the metal that the hull is comprised of. The first step, of course, is to clear…"

Vahns was interrupted by Terry, "Commander Vahns, I don't know diddly-squat about science. I only know computers. Speak in English that I can understand."

"Very well, sir. Basically, we and the other ship maneuver into a belly-to-belly position to one another. At a crucial juncture and distance, we reverse the magnetic fields that causes a magnet to stick to us. Basically, we're becoming two North poles on a magnet, thus repelling us. At that point, our magnetic fields that are generated will create a sparkle, in a matter of speaking, and bounce the ships away from us. In that critical instant, we can transport through armor plating or shields using flash technology."

"That still wasn't plain English, but that'll have to suffice." Terry said, accepting the lengthy explanation. "What happens if we adjust the field stronger than the required limit?"

"We basically bounce the other ship away from us in the opposite direction at an alarming rate."

"They will survive though, right, given the ship we're about to encounter and do this procedure with is about the size of the assassinated President's convoy?"

"Yes, sir, but it would take a lot of effort. Do you plan on doing this, sir?"

"Yes,"

"It is my duty to object, sir."

"Commander Vahns, this channel is consistently recorded, so your objection is noted. Can you do it without killing them, harming them, and getting us the hell out of here?"

Hesitantly, Vahns replied, "Yes, sir."

"Set up the procedure. Have Billy report to the Command Arena. We'll take care of the proper input procedures up here."

"Very well sir, but I must object again."

"So noted. Now send Billy's up here." Terry hit the button on the monitor to shut off the channel. He stood up and saw that everyone was staring at him. Rolling his eyes, he turned to Meghan, "Meghan, do you think Johnston believed any of that crap we told him?"

"Well, likely not, Terry, but since you sounded so convincing, it's a possibility."

"Lauren, where are we in space exactly?" Terry asked, moving on.

"We're about one hundred thousand kilometers from Earth at the moment." She responded after glancing down at her station monitor.

"Private Curtis," Terry again moved on, turning to the other science Marine officer, "how long would it take us to get to the dark side of the moon from here?"

"About four hours, sir." Curtis instantly responded, "Give or take thirty minutes."

"Terry," Randy interrupted, "we're getting in position in about four minutes."

As Terry listened to Randy, Billy walked onto the Command Arena, manning what would have been

Terry's station at Operations. He continued at the station uninterrupted as Terry was asking questions of the crew.

"So, will we be able to tap into Earth's television stations from there, since this will obviously be televised, Lt. Curtis?"

"Because we're bouncing signals off satellites and other necessary channels, it may be a little staticy with all the interference, but I think we'll manage." She responded after inputting commands on her keyboard.

"The dark side of the moon will provide us a greater interference than the bouncing off satellites will," Meghan interrupted, "Because we are hidden, so to speak, we are aiming at satellites that aren't in direct line of sight."

"We'll have to send out a buoy," Lauren added.

"Yeah, with a T5B cloak, I get that, Lauren," Terry instantly responded.

"Two more minutes," Randy informed the others of their time constraint.

"Can they trace our path, Lt. Curtis?" Terry asked again.

"Yes, but only to about fifteen minutes at Mach 5, but any telescope, even generic, will be able to see us."

"I'm talking about with the cloak, Lieutenant?"

"Our rocket trail will dissipate around the fifteen minute mark, and I was accounting for the fact that we might be cloaked. We had a cloak installed prior to our departure from the United Nations Space Station." Curtis said back quickly, as if she was getting annoyed at Terry.

"FYI, everyone, we have one more minute, guys," Randy again informed.

"Terry," Billy interrupted, "I've set the coordinates and sequence up for flawless flash sequence."

Terry walked over to Billy's station and glanced over the numbers. He then whispered commands into Billy's ear at a low enough voice where no one could here. Billy nodded in affirmation.

"Time's up, Terry," Randy said. "It's now or never."

Terry stood up straight, "Billy, engage. Once confirmation comes to your screen, Curtis, engage T5B cloak and set course for the dark side of the moon, maximum speed."

Out in space, the *Frontier*'s electromagnetic field sparkled for just an instant, and then created a loud popping sound within the interiors of both ships, signifying that it wasn't done to Johnston's expectations. His small ship reverberated violently and bounced back and started spinning like a snowball going down a hill in the opposite direction of the *Frontier*. Almost an instant later, the *Frontier* disappeared from view as it started heading toward the moon.

Red Alert sirens wailed onboard Johnston's ship as the ship went spinning almost out of control. "Sir," the Lieutenant manning the pilot station informed him, "We've lost momentary control."

"Switch to manual override." Johnston ordered.

"Switching now, sir. It'll take a minute but we'll survive the tumble. We should re-dock for maintenance."

"We don't need maintenance," Johnston said.

"We do now, sir. That maneuver fried a lot of circuits on board and it would be dangerous to pursue, even if we knew where they were going."

The monitor at the nose of their Command Arena turned on, showing incoming transmission from the Pentagon. "Admiral Johnston, come in please… Admiral Johnston, come in please." It was Admiral

Amaya from his office, trying to establish contact after watching what just happened. Both ends were experiencing flickering, but audible was fine.

"Admiral Amaya, we're fine. We're regaining control of the ship and returning to Kennedy Space Center."

"Where did the *Frontier* get a T5B cloak? It wasn't supposed to get one, if ever?"

"I don't know, Admiral," Johnston replied, "There must be some kind of conspiracy afloat with these people and we will have to the bottom of this. We will return to Earth after docking and deal with these terrorists after the trial." Johnston cut the transmission.

Amaya turned to Rustin, who was also in the office with him, "Casey, you don't know anything about this, do you?"

"Of course not, sir," Rustin replied instantly, "I am not at the proper clearance levels to get that kind of information."

Amaya turned off his monitor, sat back in his chair, took a deep breath, and let it out, remaining calm even though he was astounded by the incidents that played out in the last two days. He looked at Rustin, "I guess we'll just have to seek out those answers at the trial."

CHAPTER 6

- - - - - THE TRIAL - - - - -

"According to US Eastern Standard time, at oh-one-hundred hours, the United States Starship *Frontier*, under the command of Kristina Porter, fired upon Space Craft One, carrying the President of the United States, Larry Fischer. Gravity was lost and an assassin 'flashed'," General Cue expressed his last word facing Gabe and Brian, and continued uninterrupted, "aboard and assassinated President Fischer with a modified nine-millimeter handgun."

Cue, Gabe, Brian, a judge, Josh and an audience were in a courtroom in Washington DC. It was just like any standard courtroom seen on earth, with the prosecution to the judge's left and the defense to the right. Brian and Gabe were cuffed to the table as to prevent any unwanted escape attempts. Most of the audience were that of Navy and Marine personnel and key witnesses to be called to the stand. Armed guards stood next to Brian and Gabe and the bailiffs took their normal courtroom spots. "Today," Cue said after his opening argument, "I am here to prove that these men took part, if not led, this dreadful and shameful act that took the life of our President and Commander in Chief." As standard as the courtroom was, it was more of a debate and rebuttal setup rather than a traditional "call the witness, question him or her, and then cross exam, then move on." There was no jury as it was deemed unsuited for the situation considering the jurisdiction and the overseeing party.

Admiral Amaya was watching from his office with Casey Rustin via closed circuit television televised in the same fashion the *Frontier* had been televised: worldwide and across every network known to man.

"Why is Josh Gabe and Brian's attorney? Why didn't we get them a public defender?" Amaya.

"Because, Josh has been deemed a government expert in negotiation techniques and we still have to keep appearances that he is on this mission for a purpose. Cue suggested it as to keep hopes up for the defense regardless if he does a less than adequate job than a normal defense attorney." Rustin explained, "It also provides a little sympathy for the defense to the world so that it doesn't make the military look like the culprit trying to pin blame on just anyone."

Unsure how to take that, Amaya sighed.

In the meantime, Terry and his cohorts were hidden in the cloaked *Frontier* watching over a tapped communications channel on the other side of the moon. Their television monitor on the front gave them an image flickering, as if it was trying to get reception from a primitive antenna before the days of digital antenna and cable.

Josh, as if to surprise everyone, was prepared to try to save his friends. "I hate to point out the obvious from the beginning," he stood up from his chair, "But you said the gravity magnets unit was not working. It is not hard to guess that it would surely be hard and difficult to find the President aboard the presidential convoy once they flashed over."

"Traces of flash technology indicated they flashed directly onto the level where President Fischer was located, which was the primary deck." Cue explained.

"Okay, but wouldn't a gravity-less environment still make it difficult? It's hard to believe that they can move with ease without gravity and given the fact you had two guards around Fischer at all times, it's also hard to believe that your people are not trained in either protection or self-defense."

"We are a peaceful spaceship on a mission of truce under a flag of peace. We did not expect to be invited into space and onboard your starship to die."

"Objection," Josh immediately countered, "Everyone on Earth knows why we invited the President on board after he insisted on one last inspection. It's all in recorded transcript sent to Kennedy Space Center and was broadcasted to everyone on Earth."

"Your honor," Cue said quickly to prevent the judge from second guessing, "All of this recorded information seen on Earth and sent to Kennedy Space Center is under the direction of Admiral Amaya. The Admiral had no way of knowing about a conspiracy, should he not be involved."

"Continue," the judge overruled Josh.

"Brian Rendetti," Cue stated, turning to Brian. "Stand up, identify yourself and what you do for the record."

As Brian stood up, he spoke, "I am Commander Brian Rendetti, Director of Operations for the United States Earth System Mission, USS *Frontier*, United States Marines."

"Very well," Cue smile, "However, I did not hear a *Doctor* Brian Rendetti. Why is that?"

"That would be an obvious clue or indication that I am *not* a doctor." Brian shot back quickly.

"Careful, Commander, your wits won't get you anywhere." Cue said, and then continued further, "When you boarded the Presidential Convoy, you were carrying a field med-kit, and asked to assist the patient, President Fischer. It could be taken that you posed for a doctor." Cue explained.

"I carried a first-aid kit. Everyone knows what one is," Brian said flatly.

"You also performed CPR and mouth-to-mouth resuscitation, and still didn't revive him," Cue continued.

"Everyone also knows that CPR and mouth-to-mouth is not a guarantee to survival, a panacea of sorts. It was an instinctive thing to do," Brian again was trying to get his point across.

"So you gave him artificial respiration and didn't revive him?" Cue rhetorically asked, but then turned serious, "How many people have died with artificial respiration?"

"I wouldn't know." Brian said.

Pointing a finger at Brian, Cue almost triumphed, "Precisely Mr. Rendetti. You *don't* know. You *are* incompetent. Your CPR certification has been shown to be expired as late as two weeks ago, and therefore, had no business being aboard unless it was to make yourself look good." Cue seemed content after he said that.

"Objection," Josh had exclaimed as he stood up again.

"Cue, we are not interested in what you think. We are only interested in the facts." The judge told Cue.

"These are not opinions. Think of it this way. If you want to avoid being the suspect, what better way to do so as to do by being the hero: the good Samaritan? It is a well-known forensic fact that a criminal will interject him or herself into an ongoing investigation," Cue asked of him.

"Very well," the judge said.

"Now wait just a damn minute..." Josh shouted but was interrupted by the judge.

"Do you want to save your friends, Mr. Disinell?" The judge asked of him.

"Yes," Josh immediately answered.

"Then shut up," the judge ordered.

As if they had all rehearsed, in three different areas, on earth and in space, Josh, Terry and his crew, and Amaya and Rustin's jaws dropped at the judge's remarks.

"But..." Josh protested but was cut off again.

"Josh, I said be quiet," the judge ordered again. He then turned to Cue. "General Cue, you never answered his earlier question."

"And what question would that be?" Cue wiped what appeared to be a smirk or smile on his face.

"The gravity units were not working, as you noted. How could these men operate in such an environment?"

Now Josh had a chance, or so he thought, until someone strolled in the courtroom in a wheelchair-type mobile.

"I was sitting with the President and Sir Shanaus, when Brian and Gabe flashed aboard." The Marine military officer in the wheelchair mobile said while on the stand.

"Objection," Josh again interrupted, "Commanders Rendetti and Romero have not been identified as the assailants."

"That comment has been stricken from the record." The judge ordered the clerk who was recording the whole courtroom conversations.

The wheelchair witness spoke again, raising his hand, "Let me rephrase. I was talking with President Fischer and Sir Shanaus when two people flashed aboard. They were wearing spacesuits and shot Shanaus first, and then they shot at me while I tried to get away to get my hand pistol."

"So, could you identify these assailants?" Josh asked.

"No, they had a space helmet on with their reflective glass on, as if they were in outer space facing the sun and the reflective coating was enabled." He explained.

"But still," Josh insisted, "this is zero gravity environment we're talking about? How could they just prance and dance around and function?"

Cue stepped forward before the witness could answer, "Moving your arm and pulling a trigger is not hard to do, even in zero-g. The laws of physics apply; an object at rest remains at rest unless provoked. He studied Josh as he saw Josh's disappointed facial expression take formation.

He then took a step toward the defense table where Gabe and Brian were not sitting. "Now we turn to the lead conspirer in this matter: Gabe Romero." He looked at Gabe, hoping to get some kind of response, but only received a dead stare. "Commander Romero, stand up and identify yourself to the court and for the record."

Gabe stood up slowly and smirked as he spoke. "I am Commander Gabe Romero, First Officer on board the USS *Frontier*."

"Are you really a commander, Romero?" Cue asked suspiciously.

"Yes. Why?" Gabe immediately questioned back.

"Because," he took a second to pull some paperwork off his bench and read over them, and spoke while doing so, "United States Marines records show Commander Rendetti and his career report, but you, Romero, appear to have just shown up. It would appear that you just joined them recently, beginning rank Commander. How is that possible?"

"I was recruited for this one mission," Gabe responded nonchalantly.

"And what mission would that be, Commander Romero?" Cue asked suspiciously, finding flaws everywhere. "Would that be the mission to see if we can live on Mars as originally scheduled or a mission to have President Fischer lured onboard under false pretense and then killed on the way home?"

"Objection," Josh stepped forward, "The President invited himself onboard, and by all means, not by any one onboard the Frontier."

The judged appeared as if he was going to strike the comments, but Cue immediately spoke before the judge could do so, "You honor, records show that Commander Romero, as well as Mr. Rendetti, were involved a group known as T5B, or The Five Brats, several years ago in a small town in Texas. They terrorized people, neighborhoods, and even their own town. What kind of group is that? Vigilantes, factions, terrorists? And not only do those factors play a role. President Fischer was indeed invited to dinner by Mr. Romero himself, and at that dinner, they served alcoholic beverages. Need I go on?"

The judge spoke after listening intently, "Objection overruled. Continue."

"What mission were you specifically recruited for, Commander Romero?"

In a sarcastic wit and tone of voice, Gabe apparently did not think before he spoke, which was almost instantaneous to Cue's questioning. "Well, you see, I was originally thinking that this mission was to kick your ass, but however, in a weird turn of events, I was recruited with my friends to help save the human race. As much as I love the human race, the first would've been a better option."

Restraining himself from matching wits with Gabe, Cue nonchalantly turned around, smiling with his head almost down. As he placed his hand on his chin, he brought his face back up again after pacing in a circular pattern, and questioned, "I take it you don't like me, Commander?"

"You are correct. In actuality, I hate your guts, and if I may be frank, I wish it was you that they had shot and killed, not President Fischer."

Terry was sitting in the captain's chair, his jaw literally dropping at Gabe's remarks. "Oh my God," he said, placing his face in his hands and shaking his head, "I know he just didn't say that."

"With that attitude, the trial could very well be over," Billy Fonder said, who had been on the Command Arena the whole time as well.

"Well, Romero," Cue continued, "Do you like this administration currently in power in the White House, including me, Shanaus and the rest of the cabinet that comes with a new president such as Fischer?"

"You personally, no, but I have nothing against…" Gabe said but was interrupted by Cue.

"I see," Cue had interrupted him, "I, among others, believe that you do not and were recruited to kill," he explained.

Josh stepped forward, ready to object again, but Cue spoke quickly, holding up his hand to prevent Josh from speaking, "but my, nor anyone else's opinion, matters in a trial of facts. And facts are facts. Here's the proof." He signaled to an acquaintance, who pushed a button on a digital recorder of a sort.

"Look at everyone, especially General Cue. He shows of like he's some kind of hot shot jerk and walks around like he has a corncob stuck up his hiney hole, as if he's some super macho top gun."

"Well, he is a four star general, you know." Randy said.

"Well, thank you for that information, Captain Obvious," Gabe said, *"I didn't mean it on that level. Besides, they're all jerks, I guess… and kinda ugly. They need to be shot."* He chuckled at the last statement. Randy's and Gabe's voice was heard laughing.

"OBJECTION!" Gabe yelled out, jumping up. His being handcuffed to the defense table cause the table to rattle almost to the point of being knocked over, but the shortness of the chains to him and Brian forced him back to a seating position.

"Counselor, you will calm your client," the judge ordered Josh.

Josh glared at Gabe, who kept quiet, restraining himself for speaking another word. Josh looked at the judge and stated, "He will not outburst like that again, Your Honor."

Meanwhile aboard *Frontier*, Terry swiveled to Randy, "He said that?!"

Randy answered hesitantly, "Well… not about the part about shooting them." He didn't continue, purposefully. At that moment, Terry knew the truth.

After the courtroom calmed down from the outburst, Josh stood up, attempt to save his already-doomed friend's lives, "Your honor, I must object. Gabe himself stated he didn't like Cue, and in fact, hates him. That is an opinionated view that has already been noted and shouldn't be on the record, and Gabe would deny making such remarks under oath about killing them."

Before the judge could agree, Cue stepped forward again, "However, we need to know exactly how Commander Romero feels. He called us ugly; he called us untrustworthy; he has shown hatred and prejudice on several occasions; and most notably, his voice tells us that he had the thought of killing us. All of those can lead anyone to believe that he was out for blood to stop our colonization to Mars in one way or another, even if it meant killing President Fischer."

Josh immediately countered, "That recording was altered, your honor. According to this book we're in, we just have to look in Chapter Four and we will clearly see that Gabe's last words were 'and kinda ugly'."

"Unfortunately, Mr. Disinell, I do not have access to this book you speak of, nor do you. And since there is no jury present, I just have to sort out the facts on my own and that statement will be taken into consideration if it can be deemed as a fact." He turned to General Cue, "So if you will proceed, General."

"Now tell me, Commander," Cue immediately questioned, "were those words spoken by you?"

Again holding restraint to yell out coldly, Gabe stated as calm as he could through his anger, "Well, most of it."

"Most of it, Commander?" Cue said, almost impatiently.

"Everything but the part about shooting them." Gabe said.

"And what proof do you have that this recording is faked?"

"None other than what Josh had said."

"That was your voice, was it not, Commander Romero?"

"Yes it was," Gabe said. He really disliked this Socratic Method Cue was using.

"So, since you cannot prove this recording is altered as you and Mr. Disinell have claimed and that voice is clearly yours by your own admission, we all have to be in agree-ance that all those were spoken by you, am I correct?" Cue explained nonchalantly.

Irritated at Cue's cocky tone-of-voice, Gabe responded, "I do not claim those last words spoken by me involving the shooting. I clearly remember stopping at the word 'ugly' and I will stand by that testimony."

"Yes you will, Commander Romero, but the honorable judge here will determine what truth is and what is not during his deliberation." Cue explained, once again giving a cocky tone of voice.

"Get to your argument, General," The judge ordered.

Cue's smile drained from his face, or so it seemed. "Very well. I do have a few more questions, Commander Romero." He paused but only for a second, as if to gather his thoughts, "Were you ever in command of the *Frontier*?"

"Briefly," Gabe said, almost immediately.

"Who is now in command?" Cue asked.

"Lieutenant Commander Terry Farran," Gabe said, his facial expression now in an expressionless state.

"Wait a minute," Cue pointed up a finger, "what happened to Captain Kristina Porter?"

Gabe thought quickly, wondering what Terry might say, "She uh," he stalled.

"She uh what, Commander?" Cue asked impatiently.

"Died during your attack," While not knowing it, he had directly quoted Terry.

Terry, who had his chin on his fist while sitting in the chair watching what they all thought was a show-trial, whispered to himself, "Damn! He's good!"

Cue turned away from Gabe, slowly walking to his seat where his files were located, "Commander Romero, what if I told you Commander Farran said differently?"

"Why would we tell two different stories when there is only one?" Gabe immediately responded, as if he was prepared for the question.

"You are correct, Commander Romero. There is only story. You are also right in saying that I was wrong. Terry did, in fact, say exactly what you said he said, siding with you, but here's where you're wrong. We have this awesome, not-so-secret technology even your average city police officer uses. It's called infrared technology. Coupled with other technologies, like sonar, that the United States and other national governments use, we can run a detailed scan of any object in space, especially on within close proximity of Earth, say, between the Earth and the Moon."

"Get to the point, General," the judge ordered.

"The point of me explaining that to you, Commander Romero is that according to our own sensor scan of the Frontier while it was stationary after the attack on the President revealed something very interesting." Cue explained.

"I am sure it was exciting," Gabe smirked.

"Well, it was, Commander," Cue faked a smile. He picked up an electronic tablet off his desk and tossed it on the table Gabe and Brian were sitting at. He had aimed well, as it slid to a stop in front of Gabe. "Read it, Commander Romero, and tell the court what it says."

Gabe glanced at the pad, as it had a diagram with military code words on scribbled in typewriter text on it. "I can't read this crap," he stated, glancing back up, "it looks like a map or diagram with these stupid code words you use."

Cue and the judge frowned at Gabe's remarks. Cue reached toward Gabe, pushed couple of buttons on the tablet, and an instant later, it turned to proper English.

"Now," Cue said, "tell the court what it says."

Gabe leaned forward this time, reading the text that was displayed next to a diagram of the *Frontier*. "Life sign in Room 35 Active. Door locked and life sign restrained. Security posted outside."

"Good, Commander, now whose room is Room 35 designated for; that is, on the *Frontier*, for whom is this room specifically designated for?"

Again, Gabe had to restrain to prevent the Socratic Method Cue was using from drawing out an outburst. "Captain Porter," Gabe said, rolling his eyes, knowing all too well what was to come.

"How about that!" Cue triumphed while Josh placed his face in his right palm. Cue continued uninterrupted, "Captain Kristina Porter locked in her quarters and restrained." Gabe growled at him while he picked up his tablet and turned the other way to walk over and hand the tablet to the judge. "May I present Exhibit A, your honor," walking toward Gabe very slowly, he continued while the judge looked over the evidence.

"Let me tell everyone what has happened here, your honor. T5B has returned, this time with a vengeance. With Gabe's help, they organized the greatest crime in American history so profound it will be remembered for generations to come. This plan was set in motion by the false invitation of President Fischer to assess his security measures. It was then further invoked in the mutiny of the USS Frontier, *and then firing upon our ship and the assassination of the Commander in Chief. In hopes of escaping and going unnoticed, they offer assistance aboard the President's escort and have Terry Farran lie for them. Finally, Gabe lies to protect his friends, proving that we cannot believe anything he says because we now know it could be a lie. Gabe, your honor, is our lead conspirer, if not the assassin himself. And Brian, a fellow conspirer trying to pose as something he is not, again in hopes of covering the truth."* Cue walked back to his desk, and sat proudly, *"Your honor, the state rests."*

The judge walked into the courtroom and everyone stood up formally. As he sat down, so did everyone else. There was an eerie silence in the room, as if they were walking into a known haunted house.

The judge took a second to organize paperwork on his desk, looked up, and then spoke, mostly looking at the duo of Gabe and Brian.

"Gabe Romero and Commander Brian Rendetti, this has been a very unique case, considering the circumstances. There is no precedent for such a trial for a case of this magnitude. It has been very difficult to access the facts, the circumstances, and the video recordings of all pertinent events over the last couple of weeks, including the actions taken by the defense and the prosecution. And because of the magnitude of the situation, I have concluded that all evidence against you two is entirely circumstantial, with the exception of a few details and facts. It is however unfortunate that there is more evidence against the both of you than there is in defense of you two, which does not allow for any exoneration of any sort. Because the main plotline of this book, as well as this subplot, hinges on the necessity of your conviction, I have no choice but to find you guilty as charged, the crime being the assassination of President Fischer, conspiring to assassinate a government officer, misuse of government property, espionage against the United States Marine Corps, and treason against the United States of America."

Cue frowned. Perhaps he was hoping for a more overwhelming decision.

"Treason against the United States is punishable by death, and in some states, so is first-degree murder. This is not a state matter where they get to choose. This is a federal trial under the jurisdiction of the United States government as a nation. In light of the circumstances, I have no choice but to impose the death penalty."

Terry, who had not moved from the captain's chair, and still had his chin on his face. The only noticeable changes that he made were the tightening and clenching of his jaw. Lauren and Meghan were crying, tears streaming down their faces.

"However, due to the nature of this mission, the sentence of death is delayed. I must allow time for the military to convene on their own time in a classified location to discuss the matter of Mars colonization and testing. I will allow thirty days for the military commanders assigned to the situation to convene, to at which time I will then decide on a formal firing squad date. This court is adjourned." The judge finished in finality.

CHAPTER 7

---PLANS OF ACTION---

"Wow," Billy said aboard the Frontier, "so much for trial by jury."

Randy turned his head toward Billy, "and a little too graphic in describing their sentence. They might as well patch an entire visual across all television channels on Earth."

"Randy, Billy, shut up. Gabe and Brian are innocent and shouldn't have to go through this," Meghan snapped, in turn receiving stares from everyone except Terry, who still had his chin on his fist. She then stormed to the elevator, and Lauren followed her. Meghan dropped herself to the elevator floor, wrapping her arms around her bent knees, crying as she leaned her head on the opposite door. Lauren knelt down to console her as the doors closed shut.

As everybody except Terry watched sympathetically, moments of uneasy silence followed, and for a few more brief moments, no one dared to speak.

"Randy," Terry said, looking and obtaining correct chair posture.

Quickly, Randy turned to Terry.

"Who could have fired those missiles?" Terry asked almost uninterrupted.

"Upon review, only us. Unless they came out of thin air," Randy responded immediately.

"Hardly relevant, Mr. Randy, since outer space has no air." Terry responded just as quickly.

"You know what I mean, butt wipe," Randy shot back, showing he did not intend to explain himself.

"Well, Mr. Randy," Terry said, pushing himself to a standing position, "As you put it, either we fired, or 'thin air' fired. Billy," he said, turning to Billy, "What exactly is 'thin air'?"

"Well, air is thinner at higher elevations on earth, such as in places like Denver or mountain ranges at their peaks as opposed to places like Miami, Florida or Corpus Christi, Texas. Air, in and of itself, is composed of a mixture of nitrogen and…"

"BILLY!" Terry called out, interrupting him.

"And invisible ship," Billy said quickly, "Come on, man! Lighten up. I was trying to be funny."

"Is that possible?" Stacey Norton asked, interrupting the conversation.

"Lt. Norton," Randy intervened, "Billy is *never* funny, so no, that isn't possible."

"I meant the invisible ship explanation Officer Fonder offered." Stacey said, annoyed at the fact T5B were being sarcastic and funny in the light of a very real threat. To her, it didn't seem like this group didn't take the situation seriously at all.

"That doesn't make sense, Lieutenant, since we are using the T5B cloak right now, which makes us almost entirely invisible." Randy explained, serious this time.

Lt. Norton still had a puzzled look on her face.

Rolling his eyes, Randy shook his head and turned to Billy, ignoring her, "Billy, you sure we didn't fire those missiles?"

"I counted each and every one of our missiles personally with Commander Vahns' witness verification and I did it accurately, so yes, we have every missile according to our load and roster specifications as set forth in the inventory list."

Terry took the moment to rejoin the conversation, "Tell me, Mr. Randy, when you all were as a group and Gabe returned to Perryton for the second round of T5B when I was the enemy, was he invisible when he fired those explosives?"

"I never saw his car until afterwards when I turned around after passing the railroad tracks."

"So in conclusion," Billy said, "we're dealing with a similar cloak like Gabe's, with the same capabilities: able to fire when cloaked. We all know that T5B's cloak wasn't meant to do such a thing."

"You are correct, Mr. Billy," responded Terry, "in this case, their cloak has a bad case of indigestion, because it sure does release a lot of gas."

Billy burped, "Me, too," he said, holding his stomach.

"And unlike you, Billy," Randy countered Billy, "this can be detectable because it gets the chance to kill."

"So," Terry said, sitting back in the command chair, "we need to quit making jokes and get to the point of this mystery. We have a murderer and/or conspirer aboard this ship. Whoever that person is needs to be caught, along with their weapon."

Randy looked at Terry, and then asked, "How do we know that weapon is still onboard? What if he or she flashed aboard the conspirer ship?"

"You're missing one important detail, Mr. Randy," Terry noted, "the person who fired those missiles may not be onboard, but the person who altered our computers still has to be. Flash technology logs indicated that flashing technology was in effect during our supposed attack on the President's ship, but have not been used since. So, whomever the assassin, he or she is still onboard, and the only question is who?"

"And the *whereabouts* is the weapon," Randy concluded.

"Exactly," Terry triumphed, "And what weapon would that be, Lt. Norton?" Terry asked, as if were a teacher prompting a student.

Stacey Norton snapped from her daze, and then looked at Terry, "A nine millimeter handgun, standard issue."

Terry turned to Randy, "Let the search begin."

Gabe and Brian were escorted in handcuffs down a narrow hallway by security guards, the same bailiffs that were there with them with leaving the courtroom. They didn't have handguns; they nudged them along with pen-like weapons. After pushing them into a dark, white-walled cell of a sort, presumably one used for solitary confinement for the darkest of criminals, the door shut behind them, and the guards tagged along in the room.

The handcuffs popped off, as if they were programmed with some microchip to release. After studying their hands for a minute or so, Gabe and Brian dared not speak, even to each other.

Without warning, the room shimmered around them and the entire environment was replaced by what could be described a super-humid, muggy rainforest. But in this rainforest, they were in an opening between the fields of forestry. Instantly, Gabe and Brian began to feel sweaty and sticky from the humid environment. The guards turned around and walked away from them, disappearing as if they were a mirage ten or so meters away while walking away.

"What the hell..." Gabe mouthed to Brian without speaking.

"More like 'where the hell are we'?" Brian said, almost chuckling.

"Feels like Hell to me," Gabe said.

"Or maybe the Hunger Games," Brian laughed.

"Yea, I suppose you're gonna have to die first," Gabe said, playing along, making light of the situation as well. "Seriously, where do you think we are? This is too real to be a simulation of a sort."

"You mean like a Star Trek Holodeck?" Brian asked.

"Well, it's obviously not since that's a totally different piece of fiction. I think they have transported us somewhere, with a technology like, if not *the* technology, to our flashing one." Gabe explained.

"Well at least they have us these uncomfortable prison boots to hike along with," Brian said, kicking a rock. "Let's take a walk; maybe we can find shelter or make some nearby." They started toward the forest ahead of them when the ground started to shake, as if an earthquake had begun. After several seconds, it was too unsafe for them stay standing, so both Gabe and Brian steadied themselves to a sitting position.

The clearing in front of them split open and opened like a platform revealing something coming from the ground. Slowly, but surely, a wide but one story building rose from the ground. The building had no windows and what appeared to Gabe and Brian as the front of the building, a door shimmered into view, as if was uncloaking.

Two men walked out and guarded the door, and a military commander of sorts, appeared. He held up a handheld CB-type speaking device, aimed at Gabe and Brian.

His voice came over loud speakers in a booming, disembodied voice, "What's your favorite scary movie?" He asked.

"I think you have the wrong storyline, buddy," Gabe said. Brian tried to laugh, but the mugginess and severe humidity of the air caused him to cough.

"Oh, right. Sorry, let me try that again," He spoke once more, this time more demanding, "Welcome to the Amazon, Gabe Romero and Brian Rendetti."

"The Amazon?" Gabe asked.

"Yes, Gabe, the Amazon. We are roughly fifty kilometers South of Leticia, in Brazil. Leticia is right on the three points that border Brazil, Columbia and Peru. To your east are the Andes and basically anywhere else are indigenous tribes willing to kill you for cannibalistic or other purposes, so right now this prison is your safest haven. Even if you did escape, there are poisonous snakes and other deadly creatures and insects that roam these forests, so it would be wise for you to listen to us, as you are destined to spend the rest of your lives here. As long as you do what you're told, you will be treated well."

Gabe looked at Brian, raising an eyebrow, "Treated well?"

Brian smirked, "Yeah, meaning brutal discipline, bad food and all the Amazonian women to your heart's content." They both turned back to the commander.

"What's your name?" Gabe asked.

"You don't need to know. But right now, you have a choice; either follow me, or stay out here to die," He gestured to someone inside, and moments later, four guards piled out with their weapon of choice, the same pen-like weapon that their former guards were nudging them along with.

"Your weapons are not very imaginative," Brian said, not impressed.

"Mr. Rendetti," the commander spoke again, "would you like an example of how this weapon works?"

"No, thanks, I think I'm content on the mystery of it." Brian responded back, hoping he would just blow his comments off.

The commander motioned one of his guards to do something. The guard went inside and pulled out a prisoner. He was obviously a troublemaking prisoner, as he was dressed in only rags and severely beaten and showing scarring all over his body. He was holding himself as the guards tossed him onto the ground.

"Give the order, sir," the guard spoke.

"The order is given," the commander said smugly.

The guard pointed the pen weapon at the prisoner. The tip of lit up, but nothing seemed to happen, until the prisoner that was the target started to melt. He let out a terrible scream, one that neither Gabe nor Brian had ever heard before; one that sent a chill down their spines. Gabe and Brian stood there, stunned at the sight and the hair on the backs of their necks stood up on ends. There was nothing visible that they could see: no energy, no string, or tazer-lik tip, just the glowing end of the pen weapon. Roughly fifteen seconds later, the prisoner was reduced to a pile of melted human flesh and crystalized bone.

"Just remember," the commander reminded them, "you could our next example, so I advise you to do what you're told." He walked back into the hallway that the door led to and disappeared, leaving everyone behind. The guards gestured for Gabe and Brian to move inside, and they did exactly as they were told, knowing what their fate might be if they didn't.

Randy and Lauren walked into the ship's bar, which was designed to look like a sport's bar. Terry was already sitting at the bar, sipping a drink. "Terry," Randy started, "we have the entire crew aboard looking for the gun."

"But the killer could be any one of them," Lauren finished.

"There has to be an easier way," Terry said after taking his sip, "this ship only goes to Deck F."

"The ship may be small, but searching the ship ourselves would take at least two or three weeks at the very least." Randy said.

"Small, Randy?" Terry asked, "According to the standards of this time, this ship is not small. It is huge, and expensive. I was just more apprehensive at the fact we have over a hundred people searching for the gun, so it shouldn't take that long."

"Well still," Lauren added, "our evidence is bound to escape our sight in some way or another. It's like looking for your car keys while in a rush out the door, when in fact, they are right in front of you on the coffee table. Besides, someone's bound to move it or conceal it somehow without our knowledge."

"Is there not someway to dispose of this gun by now?" Randy asked.

"This is not Earth, Mr. Randy. This is a spaceship in outer space we're talking about," Terry explained, taking another sip, "They can't just throw it out the window, dump it in a garbage can down the street or take it to some buddy's house temporarily."

"I see your point," Randy said.

"What about the recycling unit? Perhaps there might be an operative there." Lauren offered.

"Good idea, Lauren," Terry said, "You and Meghan get down there and search the area. Get Private Curtis to get you a composition recorder so you can see what types of recycles are in there. If the gun's recycled, then you will be able to tell with that."

"Okie dokie," Lauren said, turned the other way and walked out of the bar.

As she left, Billy had walked in and walked toward them. He leaned on the bar and told the bartender, "Crown Coke please."

Both Terry and Randy studied Billy, and simultaneously cracked a smile. Terry whispered to Randy, gesturing with his drink, "Seems like Crown Coke is the choice of drink around here."

After Billy got his drink, he took a few more steps and join Terry and Randy. "Well," he started, "if this is not a page from the past."

"A torn page, that is," Randy said.

"Billy, I understand that you and Commander Vahns are having difficulties getting our engines working and the docking clamps," Terry told Billy.

"Actually, they're working fine, Terry."

"No… they're not," Terry said, offering no explanation.

"Okay, I'm confused," Randy said, butting in. Billy shrugged.

"If our engines are working fine and the docking clamps are not giving you trouble, then we have no reason to hide out here in the shadows and find Gabe and Brian. That means we return to Earth and go about our merry way. Comprende, amigo?" Terry said, taking yet another drink, this time finishing his drink and setting the glass on the counter.

"Well," Billy said, "we are experiencing an unknown issue with the engines. It could take time to figure that out. As for the docking clamps, if we don't get them fixed, we'll never be able to dock back to the space station and get off this ship safely."

"Doing so could cause implosion, or worse, destroy the ship," Randy offered.

"How long would it take, Billy?" Terry asked.

"A week, at the very least," Billy said.

"Good for you, Mr. Billy," Terry said, and continued. "Now it's time to go solve this mystery."

In the prison, Gabe and Brian laid on the metal beds where they were assigned to sleep. They only had prison scrubs on, their only attire given to them, plus a couple of pillow-type cushions. Gabe tossed and turned, trying to sleep, but couldn't, so he just kept his eyes closed.

Brian was lying on the bunk above him. They shared a large room with other prisoners, a room that reminded both of them of military barracks. He peeked down to Gabe, and started talking, "Gabe?"

Gabe opened his eyes, but didn't move, staring at the wall in which the bunk was mounted to, "What?"

"I'm sorry, Gabe."

Gabe shifted to a seating position, looking up to Brian, literally. "For what?" He asked.

"Everything," Brian continued to show only his head, and the tops of his fingers, which his hands were gripping the edge of the bunk. "You were right. Who was I to think of bringing you guys on this mission?"

"I don't know," Gabe said, pausing a second, "perhaps maybe it was for the best that it was us, instead of some other person here with you right now."

"No, Gabe, that's not the point. I know we haven't shared a pretty past together, regardless of you, Brooke or any other event that took place afterwards. I wanted to share history with my friends, just not this kind of history." There was almost a hint of sarcasm in his voice at the last statement, and the left corner of his mouth moved upward, as if to smirk.

Gabe laid back down, putting his hands behind his head, giving himself additional neck support to his generic pillow cushion, "Don't be so hard on yourself, Brian. I didn't make events much easier for you, since I was quite the jerk there for a while with my resentment."

Brian shook his head, "Gabe, we are making history as we speak. Imagine what the headlines are now all over the world. We are now completely infamous. It's outrageous."

"Well, Brian, you're not the only one who should apologize. I had no right to be the biggest jerk on the planet to you or outburst like I did at you several times or hold grudges just because of the past. I'm sorry; I truly am. But now, it's what we do now to prove our innocence that will keep us from living in infamy."

"Well, still," Brian insisted, "it was wrong that I used my position of power to volunteer you guys. I should've at least asked you first, before ordering you all to do it."

There was a momentary silence while Gabe thought a moment, and then he spoke, "Are you afraid of what's to come?"

The corners of Brian's mouth showed a slight smile, "I think that's one of the points I was trying to get across to your thick skull."

"No," Gabe said, shaking his head, "not that."

Instantly, Brian's smile disappeared, "What is this: an effing pop quiz?"

Gabe chuckled, and then continued, "No, you imbecile, not what's going to happen here, or the fact that we may end up like some green Nickelodeon slime goo, but what's to come in the lines of hate and prejudice."

"What do you mean?" Brian asked, curious.

"I set the example," Gabe explained, "of how we're supposed to act aboard the starship sent to save the human race. I showed hate, prejudice, and the like. What are people supposed to think now? I don't know how to explain it further, but you get the picture. Plus, this whole thing. I smell a set up."

"First, you told me a few minutes ago to not be hard on yourself. You should take your own advice. Second, I think the set up idea is pretty original. Somebody went to great lengths to take us out, tarnish our name, kill our president, and who knows what else."

"Yeah," Gabe sighed, "and the sad thing is, is that I don't know havé a clue where to go from here. I mean, what the hell, man?"

Brian chuckled more, then continued, "Well regardless. Let's just put our past in the past where it belongs and find a way out of here."

"Ha," Gabe replied, "Good luck with that."

As if timing was precise, someone walked into the barracks from about fifty meters away. Quickly, Gabe and Brian glanced in the direction and instantly positioned themselves into sleeping positions, pretending to be asleep. Gabe clenched his fist.

For a few silent seconds, nothing was heard. Just before Gabe was about to open his eyes, someone, or something, tapped Gabe. Instantly, Gabe swung his free arm, intending to hit whoever had tapped him, but whoever it was, caught his fist just as quickly. It appeared to be a muscular fellow prison inmate, approximately the same height as Gabe.

With his other hand, the man placed his finger across his own mouth in the hush position as he glanced around suspiciously. After he made sure the coast was clear, he spoke in soft whisper, "You cannot imagine the torture that goes on in this place. They promise to treat you well, but instead torture you on a daily basis. It's their way of getting their kicks on the rejects of society."

Gabe squinted his eyes, as if he was annoyed. He glanced right, then left, and then back to the guy, still holding his fist. The guy let go of his fist. Gabe spoke, "Who are you and why are you here?"

"Because I know who you are, Gabe?" the man spoke to him, "we all hear the guards speak the gossip on all prisoners and why they get sentenced here."

"This seems fishy," Gabe instantly said, almost in an accusing voice.

"Lower your voice, Gabe. Someone might here you." The man said.

"I don't care," Gabe continued to get more annoyed. "Why are you here?"

"Well, first of all, it's not every day we get the assassin to a United States President and second of all, the guards seemed to make sure we all overhear them."

Brian peeked back from the top bunk, "There's more to this, isn't there?"

"Yes," the man said, "there is. It's not only Brian's choice to send your group on this mission. It's a whole conspiracy to have you all dead. Your friends are now next."

"How do you know about all of this?" Gabe said.

"Because I'm a trustee." The man replied, "I get more inside information than the average prisoner. I have access to government libraries, computers which means…" he let his voice fade away.

"Which means what?" Brian asked.

"Which means I can help you two escape." The man replied again.

"Oh wow, like we didn't see this conversation coming," Gabe said snidely.

"Shut up with your sarcasm, Gabe." The man said. "Just know that I have read and overheard everything about you, and that I want to get out of here as much as you do. If you don't believe me when I say they torture you, then you can have a nice, pleasant view of my whip marks and scars on my back in the daylight when we're working. The thing is, I know you have to have some sort of plan to get out of here."

Gabe glanced at Brian, who gave him a look that told him that this might be their only way out. Gabe looked back to the man. But before Gabe could speak, the man spoke again, "Just report for work duty in Section Beta 12 tomorrow morning when they wake you up. Ask for Direse, your supervisor."

Gabe turned to look at Brian, "Are you ready for this?"

"It's worth a try." Brian agreed.

Gabe turned back to the man, who appeared to have slithered away in the darkness. He then turned in the direction of the door and saw a shadow sneak out of the room. Almost irritated, Gabe turned back to Brian, "Really?" He threw his hands up in the air.

"Really what?" Brian asked back.

"That's a rhetorical question, dumbass." Gabe then plopped back down, closed his eyes, and fell back to sleep.

CHAPTER 8

---PLANS IN ACTION---

Terry walked with Randy down a corridor aboard the *Frontier*. "Well, Randy, what do you think?" he asked of him.

"I don't know. It seems like we're taking an awfully long time to find this conspirer, or whoever the hell he or she is. The more time we take finding justice provides whoever it is sufficient time to hide or dispose of the gun."

"Do you think we should just give up and go get Gabe?" Terry asked.

"Nah, not yet. We don't want to show that kind of giving up attitude to whoever's on board." Randy countered.

Terry nodded to agree as he and Randy walked into a greenhouse. The greenhouse was on the very back end of the ship on Deck A, with proper lamps strategically placed around the room. The walls and ceiling were made out of special glass so that they could maintain the proper humid temperature. It was at that point Lauren met them.

"Here are the readings that I have found from the composition recorder," she told Terry, handing him an electronic tablet.

"This tells me that all recycles were only cans and paper and other similar junk like that," Terry replied after a moment of studying the readout.

"Well, yeah, that's what it says," Lauren said in a voice imitating a high school head cheerleader seen in a teen movie.

"Well, so much for that idea," Randy said. He started walking in further, and Terry followed. Terry and Lauren had only walked in the door a couple of steps when they heard a gunshot. Immediately, Terry turned around and pushed Lauren out the door with as much force as he could muster, sending her falling backwards into the corridor. An instant later, with no time to see if she was okay, he slid the door shut and locked it by hitting the lock image on the electronic console. Randy had already jumped to the ground, taking cover. Terry followed his lead.

They started crawling through an aisle in the greenhouse, "Randy, who is it?" Terry whispered loudly.

Randy sprang into the air, leaping like a frog from one lily pad to another. He fell into the cover of the tables and plants as another gunshot rang out, shattering nearby flower pots. Even during the split second he could see who it was, he couldn't tell who it was because the person had a device that emitted a force field in front of him or her that obscured his or her features. Randy whispered back as Terry crawled toward him, "I don't know. It looks like I'm trying to look through a shower door. It might take a minute or two to focus completely, but by then, I'd be history."

They crawled further toward the back of the greenhouse when the person stepped into the aisle they were in. Instantly, with cat-like reflexes, Terry and Randy got up and jumped in opposite directions, knocking over plants and hurtling over tables.

"Terry!" Randy yelled.

"What?!" Terry screamed back to him as bullets seemed to spray everywhere and pots continued to be shattered all over the place. He had jumped in the process of yelling his response back to Randy as he crashed into a small rose bush. "Ouch," he said in response.

"T5B Code 38 to window," Randy finished.

"Okay, but Code 67 while 38 is underway," Terry instantly yelled back.

"Understood," Randy said, standing up while getting sprayed with dirt and broken flower pot shards. "Hey over here!" he yelled to the gunman. As expected, the gunman shot in his direction, narrowly missing him. "Whoa!" Randy yelled to himself, jumping back to the ground. Randy whispered again to himself, "I always have to be the one dodging bullets," He started scooting across the floor, just in time to avoid another bullet. "I hate this risking my life business. I think I should work for Gabe at Sonic when we get back." Randy was able to get the attention of the gunman, leaving Terry to perform what had to be done.

"Command Arena!" Terry whispered into his walkie-talkie after grabbing it from his belt clip.

"Command Arena here," Meghan responded back over the walkie-talkie. Terry could barely hear of the noises of the gunshots, which apparently seemed to never end as it was apparent the person had a lot of clips with him or her.

He continued uninterrupted though, "I'm preparing to engage T5B Code 38 to greenhouse windows and the instant I engage, seal off greenhouse. Understand?"

There was a momentary pause before she responded back, "Uh, what the hell is T5B Code 38?" Meghan's voice asked.

Terry, not one for this type of patience, quickly yelled back, "Damn it, ask Billy. He knows."

Again there was another momentary pause before she came back on, "Understood. T5B Code 38, but I don't like it."

"Tough," Terry yelled back again, covering his head to prevent shards of broken flowerpots from hitting him in the back of his head, "Cry me a river later, but it's already set in motion. Terry threw his walkie-talkie to the ground and then crawled toward a set of windows.

"Ow-eee!" Randy yelled, spinning to the ground after getting a bullet in the shoulder. He fell to the ground, stunned, holding his wound. He then tried to get up with his other hand after a few moments but fell because of the sudden pain.

The figure approached Randy, slowly, pointing the gun at his head. This person stopped, looking down at Randy. As he or she cocked the gun for the final kill shot, Randy squinted to focus in on the identity. As he could barely start to identify, he was interrupted as he heard a yell.

"HEY! Over here!" It was Terry yelling over the sudden calmness and quietness.

The person looked away from Randy, but kept the gun pointed at Randy.

Terry had a sledgehammer type too, ready to strike the windows.

Randy eased a little to try to see the person's face, but unfortunately for him, the force field was made flawlessly to the point where it just made pixels out of the person's face.

"You shoot that gun," Terry yelled, "I will shatter these windows, and then we all die."

"That's my point," the person said in an English tongue. The voice had a mechanical tone to it, telling the duo that they weren't going to be able to tell what gender the person was, as they were using a voice synthesizer. The person then fired the gun, still pointed at Randy, and instant later, the gunman aimed at Terry and fired. Terry had already dropped the hammer and ran toward the greenhouse door that led to the rest of the ship. As each bullet hit the glass right behind Terry, the explosive decompression began.

It was only a couple of bullets and a few broken windows later that caused a chain reaction of shattering glass throughout the greenhouse. Instantaneously, glass, plants, lamps and tables were everywhere and flying around, sending them, Terry, Randy and the person out into space. The ship itself rocked with the sudden decompression on the back end of the ship, since the greenhouse was located at the tail end of the ship on Deck A.

Only moments stood before they all died in the vacuum of space.

Gabe and Brian walked along a corridor with another group of inmates. The inmates they were walking with were wearing dirty prison garb and apparently were lacking in taking a shower. The prisoners that were walking with Gabe and Brian did not pay attention to them, but like a sore thumb, they stood out to the passerby's, as they received stares from each one of them as they passed.

Gabe whispered to Brian as they were walking, "Is this really a prison? It sure doesn't look like one."

"I think so, Gabe," Brian said, "But everyone here seems to be more robotic and utopian, as if they are acting the part, or drugged to act that way. Maybe we are guinea pigs in a laboratory of a sort."

"Yeah, maybe we get to become genetically engineered. Do you think they've kidnapped all these people and are performing some kind of experiments on them or something?"

"Ha ha ha," Brian said. He then stopped, as did Gabe. "I think this might be it." He pointed to a sign above the door that read 'diversão'. "My Portuguese might be off a bit though."

"Well, let's hope this is it, then," Gabe said as he led the way into the room and looked around for a few moments.

The room was a large one, about the size of a football field. The room was almost crowded and there were tables all around. It seemed as if they stepped into a comedy club, where the stage was in the far distance and all the tables spanned out from it and were strategically placed across the room. It seemed as if there were prisoners sitting down and enjoying a drink, but they were neatly dressed in clean prison garb, rather than the dirty ones Gabe and Brian walked with. Somebody on stage was singing.

"I think we found the recreational facilities instead," Gabe said, turning to Brian.

The man on stage finished his song. He was at such a distance that Gabe or Brian couldn't make out his features. He had apparently finished his song because of the applause that came from the crowd. After the applause subsided, he spoke in great clarity that it echoed throughout the room where even Gabe and Brian could hear clearly, "Obrigado. Muito obrigado."

Brian leaned forward to Gabe, "I believe he said, 'thank you. Thank you very much' with an accent."

"And just who does he think he is: Elvis Presley?" Gabe countered immediately.

Suddenly, they noticed two security guards with walkie-talkies heading in their direction from the right side of the room. They were talking in the walkie-talkies as they headed towards the duo.

"Time to go," Brian said, pulling Gabe toward the door and into the hallway. "It was the recreation hall. Diversão means entertainment. I can't believe I missed that."

"You can't tell me that was really Elv…" Gabe said but stopped immediately as they both ran into two security guards that came up from behind them, different guards than the ones that they saw heading over to them.

"Vem com a gente," One of them spoke in a deep voice.

Gabe looked at Brian, shrugged, and then turned back to the man who asked him something. He spoke in slow enunciation, and in Spanish, "No ha-blo por-tu-gués."

The two men looked at each other for a second, then they grabbed them, as if they were bouncers at a club fixing to send someone out the door. They started to lead them away, but this time, they were interrupted by someone else.

Brian whispered to Gabe in the middle of the men's conversation. "He said in Portuguese, 'come with us', stupid. You really should learn the right language."

The single man who interrupted Gabe, Brian and their escorts spoke to the other two, "Estoy tomando desde aquí."

Brian, in turn, whispered to Gabe, "He said he's taking us from here."

The other two men paused for a second, and then left. The single man held up an electronic box of some sort and spoke Portuguese into it. The voice chirped back at them in English, "Gabe, correct?"

"Uh, yes, sir," Gabe replied slowly.

"I am Direse."

"Well, thanks for saving us," Gabe said.

"Oh be quiet, and quit walking into places you don't belong." Direse was speaking English now that the other two had left. He turned the other way, and Gabe and Brian followed. In what seemed like a very long walk to Gabe, somebody stopped in front of them, blocking all three of them.

"O que você está fazendo com eles aqui?" The man asked Direse.

Brian again leaned closer to Gabe and whispered the translation, "Something about what is he doing with us here."

"Estou levando-os para limpar esgotos," Direse said immediately and formally and Brian in turned translated to Gabe, "I think he said he taking us to clean sewage or something like that."

The supervisor, who was dressed in military uniform of unknown origin, nodded, and pointed into a direction to Gabe and Brian's right.

"Great," Gabe whispered to Brian, "we get to do crap."

"It's always what I wanted to do, but not this literal," Brian quipped back in response to Gabe's humor.

After walking down a long hallway in the direction the supervisor sent them, they came upon a wall.

Brian looked at Gabe, "Well, what are you standing around for? Start cleaning your crap up."

Gabe chuckled, "Now what?" he asked Direse.

"Only this."

Instantly, Gabe, Brian and Direse were spun in a half-circle. Gabe and Brian, not expecting the movement, fell off the pad that rotated. After they cleared their heads, they looked up, and now saw nobody except Direse. The floors and walls were apparently a dirt tunnel dug into the earth and the air was more humid than they ever encountered in their lives. Instantly they began to start to sweat as the muggy atmosphere made them sticky with sweat.

"Where are we?" Gabe asked, adjusting his collar and shirt.

"We have opened a secret door to an underground tunnel exit." Direse explained, picking up a duffel bag of a sort off the floor that apparently had been previously put there beforehand. "You were also spun around so fast you couldn't keep equilibrium or balance, so in turn, you flew off the pad. Simple inertia."

"What about you?" Gabe asked suspiciously, "We didn't see you fall or get up."

"It's called experimental medications that help give you better abilities than the average human already has."

"Uh huh," Gabe said, not believing him.

"Whatever," Brian interrupted, "Let's just find a way out of here."

Direse threw the bag over toward Gabe and Brian, "There are some canteens in there with water and prison food ration baggies. Trust me, we will need them, all of us."

Gabe picked up the bag and threw the strap over his shoulder, "I'll carry first, then you can, Brian."

Direse stepped forward and led the way, "Let's go."

They walked for about a mile and what seemed like forever, Direse, Gabe and Brian came upon the exit of what appeared to be a forest. The sun was just behind them to the East, as it was rising. The air was humid and muggy, just as it was in the tunnel. Being in that part of the rainforest, Gabe and Brian knew they had an incredible journey ahead of them, provided they survived.

Brian grabbed a canteen from the bag, took a drink and shared with Gabe. After putting the canteen strap over his shoulder, Brian shrugged, unsure on what to do.

"Let's go. I know a place a few miles from here where we can hide out and for them to have difficulty locating us after they realize we're gone." Direse gestured into a Southwesterly direction toward a mountain. This mountain, just like everything else around them, was landscaped with trees, insects, animals and dangers yet to be found.

With that, Direse, Gabe and Brian headed off into the morning.

CHAPTER 9

---SEARCH & RESCUE---

One instant, Terry and Randy were being sucked out into space caused by the explosive decompression, and the next, they fell to the floor of the Command Arena. They were captured by Flash Technology and flashed to the Command Arena, put in midair since they were caught in midair.

After crashing with a thud to the floor, both Terry and Randy struggled to get up as they gagged and coughed in front of everybody on the Command Arena. After a few moments of capturing their breaths, Terry stood up. Randy remained down, holding his shoulder while coughing. Immediately several doctor's aides came and put Randy on a stretcher and started to wheel him out.

"First of all," Terry started, still recovering, "How did you escape, Randy?"

"I saw his finger on the trigger, and once I saw it move, I turned in the nick of time. He, or she, must not have seen me and pulled the trigger and aimed and fired at you." Randy explained as he disappeared into the central elevator.

The ship's doctor walked up to Terry, handing him some pills. "You should be fine, sir. Take these to help with your broken capillaries and other breathing issues. You have broken blood vessels throughout your body, so expect bruising everywhere, all right?"

"Yeah, yeah, whatever," Terry said to the doctor, almost shrugging him off.

The doctor picked up his bag and belongings, walked off the Command Arena disappeared into the far elevator.

"Okay, now why is there a greenhouse on board?" Terry said, expecting an answer. He didn't care from whom; he just wanted an answer.

Private Curtis stepped forward, who was actually behind Terry at this point, who was facing Meghan, who in turn was sitting the Captain's Chair. "Uh, Terry," Curtis said, "in case you forgot our original mission parameters, we were scheduled to see if human life could survive on Mars. The Botanicals project, a sub-mission of our original mission, was to see if our plant life could survive as well on the planet. That, Commander, is why a greenhouse is on board."

Shaking his head as if he just remembered the whole mission, Terry agreed, 'Well, okay, then," he said, "I then take it T5B Code 38 was a success?"

"Well, Terry," Meghan said, getting up to relinquish the seat, "Code 38 was actually a success… and a failure."

"Explain," Terry ordered.

"According to Billy and from I comprehend on the group's code of ethics, T5B Code 38 involves setting up a trap to nap someone, even at the risk of your own life."

"Basically," Billy explained further, "we sealed off the greenhouse with the hidden reinforced walls that are within the walls of the ship like you see in the Convoy Bay when the President boarded the ship. You lured the assailant to shatter the windows, at the risk or your lives. We basically wanted to nap this person with Flash Technology and put him or her in the brig."

Terry listened to Billy and then turned to Meghan, "You all still haven't explained anything, Meghan."

"Well the first part of Code 38 was a success, in case you haven't noticed. The room was sealed and we set the trap, which was the explosive decompression.

The second part, nabbing this killer, was not. When we flashed you out of there, they used our flash technology against us." Meghan explained.

"And what they did," Billy finished for her again. "was anticipate our next move, which means they are still one step ahead of us. We were aiming to flash them the instant after you, but they flashed the same instant we flashed you, so therefore, if we access Flash Technology logs, we will only see yours. Thus in conclusion, they escaped once again."

Everyone let out a sigh of disbelief at Billy's revelation, knowing that this hasn't, won't, and will not be an easy task to accomplish.

Several miles through the woods and several hours later in the scorching sun, Direse, Gabe and Brian were hiking in the middle of nowhere. How long they would last depended on Terry's chance of finding them in time before they succumbed to hunger, dehydration, or worse, wild, venomous creatures such as snakes or insects. Direse continued to lead the way while Gabe followed with Brian not too far behind. Direse took no effort to turn around to see if they were okay, but Gabe was different. Gabe did turn around every few minutes to make sure Brian was behind him. If he wasn't, Gabe had every intention of turning around and finding him, even if it led back to prison. Fortunately, Brian was behind him only by a couple of meters or so. Gabe turned back around, "Direse!" he yelled out.

"What?" Direse yelled from the distance. He was at such a distance apart that yelling was their only means of communication.

"How much longer?" Gabe yelled back, hoping to be heard.

"If you can see that far, look for the oddly shaped mountain rock at your one o'clock ahead. There are caves over there where we can hide out until your friends can rescue us. Of course, if we stay too long, we will die."

"GABE!" came Brian's bitter scream from behind. It was just at that moment Gabe felt a tremor of an earthquake. Stumbling, he turned around, but didn't see anybody for a moment.

"BRIAN!" Gabe called back. He steadied himself on a tree and ran back towards Brian's voice. In moments, he came upon Brian already waist deep in a quicksand pit. Brian was holding to a semi-sturdy branch from the neighboring tree, but it was a soft branch, not one for pulling someone out of a spot like that. It was crackling as it started to peel from the tree.

Thinking and reacting quickly, Gabe pulled off his shirts, the undershirt muscle shirt and the prison scrub shirt he had on top. He tied them together and tossed one end to Brian. With his other hand he grabbed another open hanging branch.

"Gabe, help me!" Brian called out.

"What the hell does it look like I'm doing?" Gabe said, smiling in the process.

Brian grabbed the shirt lying next to him and started to pull himself out as Gabe coached him, "Climb, Brian, climb."

The shirts started to rip and the tree branch Gabe was hanging on to started to tear from the tree as well. Gabe had to do something quick, or else it could lead to the death of the person he just re-friended after all these years of hostility, or both of them.

Terry pointed to a screen beside Lauren's console, "There they are," On the screen was a map zoomed into Gabe and Brian's location in South America, and a dot blinking off and on.

"How did you do it?" Stacey Norton asked, who was now on the Command Arena.

Terry smiled as he adjusted his uniform, "Simple magic," He turned around to face Billy and Commander Vahns, who were talking over a readout on another console near Randy's station. "Commander Vahns, Billy, start your engines. They seemed to have escaped sooner than we have planned."

Commander Vahns nodded as Billy smiled and spoke, "Aye aye Captain," he said mockingly, and then followed Vahns into the elevator and disappeared.

Stacey asked Terry more questions, "First, don't you think they're already out on the lookout for them, so they might have some kind of force field in place to prevent flashing. And second, aren't you scared of being seen from Earth?"

Randy stepped forward, "First off, Earth undoubtedly saw our plants fly out of the ship after the assailant attack in the greenhouse, so they are on the lookout for us, which means we have to get as far away from that location in space as we can. Secondly, as Gabe would put it, those d-bags don't know we're coming, so it would be doubtful to have some kind of force field in place to protect prisoners. Besides, they are more likely to die first from the weather and nature elements out there in South America before they get caught anyhow."

"Gabe, don't risk your life for me," Brian yelled, "This isn't a movie, so don't expect a miracle, so just quit trying."

"No, I won't," Gabe yelled back, "Movie, book or not, we're not dying way out here in the damn boonies!"

The shirt ripped further and it was seconds from coming apart at the seams. As Brian pulled further, Gabe's hand slipped further down the branch, and the branch ripping from the tree wasn't helping, either.

"Gabe," Brian said with a tear in his eye, which after a moment disappeared with the already-present sweat he had on his dirty face. "Leave me… we both don't have to die."

"NO, we don't!" Gabe insisted, slipping from one hand on the branch as he gripped Brian's hand from the shirts with the other. The branch was seconds from snapping unless Gabe let go of his grip intentionally. "My wedding band, Brian. T5B Code 52, remember? Terry told me to wear it."

At that moment, Gabe lost his grip and flew head first, as if he were trying to tackle Brian in some kind of quicksand mud wrestling match.

The *Frontier* flew toward Earth as incredible speeds. They knew that a small bulkhead of the ship was exposed from the cloak was easily seen from somebody on the lookout for them, so they had to keep on the move so that they were not a sitting duck from earth bound missiles. One the Command Arena, they could feel the vibrations of the ship, and they seemed to get worse as Billy and Commander Vahns were tweaking the engines to push it further beyond its regulated and safety limits of Mach 5.

Stacey turned around to face Terry, "She won't last much long under the strain. She'll fly apart."

"Well, okay, *Captain Obvious!*" Terry snapped back, "But we have to get within Flash Technology range to get Gabe and Brian before they die."

Billy's voice came over the walkie-talkie, "Terry, I can't guarantee that we will make it even to the space station. We're pushing it as we speak."

Terry leaned forward, "*Then push it, then!*" he yelled back to Billy over his walkie-talkie, "And get me more speed."

Randy turned to Terry from his station, "Uh, you do happen to know that speed's illegal, right?"

"Shut up, Randy!" Terry said in a serious voice, but chuckled at the same time.

Moments later, Billy's voice came on again over the walkie-talkie, "Estimated time to atmospheric Flash Technology range, is twenty minutes. If we had a measurement of speed, it would be approximately Mach 5.782 and slowly… and I mean slowly, climbing."

"Divert all power to engines, and I mean everything. Electricity, water, everything that uses power except life support," Terry ordered.

"Understood, but I don't know how much longer I can hold 'er together," Billy said with a fake, rushed Scottish accent.

What seemed like an eternity but only seconds later, Direse had appeared and had tackled Gabe as Gabe fell toward Brian. Direse and Gabe rolled for a second before Direse got back up and used a broken branch to help Brian out of the quicksand. After a minute or two, Brian was safely back on level ground, sticky and dirty from the chest down from quicksand goo.

"Why that cunning little, cold-hearted, son of a…" Brian said, referring to Gabe's comment about the wedding band and Terry himself.

"If you hadn't failed to forget the T5B Code of Conduct," Gabe said between breaths, "then you would have understood the plan from the beginning," Gabe had interrupted before Brian could curse Terry out loud even though Terry was not around to hear it.

Kneeling down with his hands on his knees slouched like he was vomiting, Brian smiled, breathing hard, "Well, I guess then I should take a refresher course."

"We don't have much time before they notice we're gone, if they haven't already." Direse said, getting up. "Let's go," he said, starting to walk off.

"Brian?" Gabe asked, helping him up.

"What's that?" Brian asked, trying to wipe the dirt off of himself, to no avail.

"This isn't a movie, but we survived anyway."

"Well," Brian said, starting to walk with Gabe in Direse's general direction. "I guess we're in real life, we're like the new Dodge Pickup. We changed the rules."

Gabe laughed, and said in a fake, deep voice, "Guts! Glory! Ram!" and then he and Brian proceeded to head off back on their journey.

Fifteen minutes later, they were at the caves Direse had led them to. Gabe and Brian took a moment to sit down, breathe, rest and share a drink from their last canteen. Direse pulled out a lantern like object from his duffle bag. Hitting a switch, it made a cackle like a bug light on somebody's front porch. After a moment, it lit up like a florescent light and lit up the darkened cave, causing bugs and insects to scatter like cockroaches to light.

Taking another drink from the shared canteen, Brian started conversation, "Thank you, for saving our lives." He passed the canteen over to Gabe.

Direse seemed to smile, "Anytime, gentlemen. If I hadn't heard you cussing and screaming at each other, then you two would be dead, and then I would be next by dehydration." He took the canteen from Gabe, stood up, drank a sip, and stretched out his arms as if he'd been in a recliner or couch all day and just stood up.

Gabe stood up as well, inching slowly to Direse to the point Direse did not notice. "We really appreciate all that you have done for us, Direse, but now I must really beat the living tar out of you." Before Direse could complete comprehension of the sentence, Gabe sucker-punched Direse square in the nose, causing him to stumble and trip backward on his own feet.

"GABE!" Brian called out, "What the hell did you do that for?"

"Oh come on, Direse," Gabe stated, ignoring Brian, "did you really think we're that stupid? Where did you get these freebie canteens and duffle bags at? And what about this lantern you got here?" He looked around suspiciously, as if he was paranoid that someone was watching him, "It's some kind of tracking system, I'm sure. What are you getting in return?"

Direse had stood up and wiped the blood from his upper lip and his bloody nose. Gabe walked up to him and gave him a slight push with both palms, "Tell me: what are you getting in return?"

"Well, I don't know the exact term for it!" Direse faded off.

"Tell us!" Brian yelled impatiently.

"Nunya," Direse said nonchalantly.

For some reason, that caught Gabe off guard, "What? What is nunya?"

"Nunya freaking business!" Direse snapped, and head butted Gabe. Gabe fell backward, and an instant later, Brian had jumped in the air and tackled Direse.

"CONGELAR!" came a voice, followed by what sounded like a gunshot. Gabe had already got back up, ready to rejoin the fight, but he stopped at the intrusion, as did Brian and Direse.

Brian got up and stood next to Gabe, whispering, "He basically told us to freeze."

"Yeah, I got that part. That's probably the only Portuguese I will probably ever understand." Gabe said.

The man who interrupted the fight pointed his pen weapon at Direse, the same pen weapon shown in demonstration to Gabe and Brian at their entrance to the prison. For a few seconds, Direse screamed in agony and pain until the life was sucked from him and he was reduced to a pile of slime and goo.

"Você está próximo!" The man called out sternly.

Again, Brian leaned a little closer to Gabe, "He said that you're next."

Gabe laughed out loud, and then spoke, "Yeah, I think I could've guessed that one, too." He then turned to the man with the pen and spoke, "Escaped convicts killed while trying to escape, huh?"

The man grabbed a translator from one of his guards that surrounded him and spoke into it, saving Brian the effort of translation, "I had to get rid of you one way or another."

"So I guess that means we're still going to die and there's no chance of negotiating a deal here?" Gabe asked.

"Sorry, bud, they told me to kill you."

"Who?" Gabe asked instantly, seeking answers.

The man spoke again after pausing, obviously taking a second to think about his upcoming answer, "Well, since I'm going to kill you anyway, you might as well know."

Gabe was hoping Terry would save them before they melted into some kind of goo from the guard's pen, so he interrupted the man, stalling for time. He then noticed something in the sky behind the guards and the man waiting to kill them. It must have been Terry firing on the prison complex with a missile or the like.

"Waiiiiiiit a second, Mr. Guard," Gabe said, holding up his hands, "at least leave me with the honor of knowing the name of the man who killed me."

The man paused again for a second and then spoke, "My name is Gerestoni."

"Well, okay, Gerestoni, I'd like to thank you for outwitting us and killing us and cutting our lives short. There was so much I had hoped to accomplish in this lifetime, but apparently that isn't going to happen now. Our Father, who art in Heaven, hallowed be thy name. Thy Kingdom come, Thy will be done, on Earth as it is in Heaven. Give us..."

"Oh, shut up!" Gerestoni interrupted, "You can tell your God in person." He turned around to his guards, tossing the pen weapon to one of them, "Kill them!" Gerestoni had turned around to his guards and started walking to exit the cave.

"Uh, sir, we cannot." One guard said.

"WHAT?!" Gerestoni said, turning around. In the split second he turned around, Gabe and Brian had disappeared and were gone.

He turned around again to the exit, only to have himself and his guards incinerated in the blast that approached them and destroyed acres upon acres of the forest in which the prison was located.

CHAPTER 10

--CONSPIRACY THEORY--

"Well, well, well," Terry said in a convoy bay to Gabe and Brian, the place that they were flashed aboard. Surrounding all of them were security guards. "If it isn't our old friends," Terry finished.

Gabe smiled, unsure on how to respond to that.

"You know," Brian said, "they were fixing to tell us who the conspirers were, but we seem to have been kidnapped."

"Yeah, well," Terry said, "you can always go back, jerk."

Brian squinted his eyes at Terry, giving him the dirtiest look he could muster up.

"Let's walk," Gabe said, walking toward the door. The security guards followed them, for good measure.

Billy was reading a technical manual in his quarters while lying down. After a few pages of skimming over schematics, he tossed the book to the side of the bed, stood up, and stretched. He then went to the sink and mirror. Placing his hands underneath the faucet, the water turned on to allow him to wet his hands.

For a few seconds, he splashed his face, grabbed a towel, and began to dry off his face.

"Man," he said to himself, "this is one long day." He then walked to the door and opened it. He took a moment as he stood in the hallway like he was going outside of his house on Earth first thing in the morning.

After a few seconds, he started walking toward the elevator, but something caught his eye. The wall panel to his left across from his quarters seem to be loose from the wall, as if one screw or anchor had popped out of its designated places. He walked over to it carefully and studied it for a second. Seeing nothing out of the ordinary, he closed his right fist and banged the panel to pop it back into place.

The instant he hit the wall panel to pop it back into place, a gunshot rang out from behind the panel, causing Billy to instantly bounce backward and onto his back. The panel had completely came off the wall as a gun the had been stowed behind it had fired. The whole vibration from the gunshot not only knocked the panel off and damaged other panels in the bullet's path, but the gun had also jarred loosed from the crook it was placed in and fell to the floor.

"Holy effing cow!" Billy screamed, staring wide-eyed at the gun, holding his hand to his chest where his heart would be. Breathing hard, he finally managed to get up and run into his room.

He grabbed some more paper towels and then came back outside and picked up the gun with the towels. He then stormed to the elevator, gun in hand, to find Terry. To someone who didn't witness or know what he was doing, he looked like a madman on a rampage, pistol in hand, but in actuality, he was searching frantically for Terry and Randy.

General Cue was in an office at the Pentagon. An officer approached him, "Sir," he said, "the complex in Brazil has been destroyed by two scud missiles. Analysis confirms they came from the *Frontier.*"

"Opinion," Cue ordered.

"I don't know sir, but Gabe and Brian were there as well. They had to have died too."

"You fool," Cue accused, "You underestimate their group; T5B is their name. DO you honestly think their friends would have let them die in the jungle?"

The officer bowed his head, not knowing what to say, "For all we know sir, they could be conspiring to let the people of the world know what really happened; it would be their effort to exonerate Gabe and Brian's escape from South America."

Cue thought for a moment, and then continued, "Analyze those findings to determine their course. We can find the location in orbit by that indirect route. As long as we get one shot on them, we can use those readings to be able to detect their emissions to pinpoint their location."

"Sir, surely they don't know that there is an emergency White House press conference telling the world of the new President's decision to continue forth the mission once they find the *Frontier*."

"If the President is to let those people off, then they would uncover what we have done to prevent this mission altogether. I think they are heading straight for the press conference with the truth, and we have to stop them."

"General Cue," the officer insisted, "surely they wouldn't risk arrest by showing up at the press conference."

"Like I said, you underestimate their group; they are going to reveal our plans. Get the limo ready so we can get to the flash site so we can board my personal convoy and destroy the *Frontier* before it reaches Earth."

"Okay, we have already figured out there is a killer and/or conspirer aboard this ship," Terry said, walking down the hallway on F Deck with Gabe and the others.

"Hmmm, my thoughts exactly," Gabe said, thinking and shaking his head. He looked up at Randy, "Um, Randy, you do know that Halloween is a few months away, so why are you dressed at Barney?" He was referring to the fact that Terry and Randy were slightly purple in color from the average human being.

Randy laughed, waving his arm, the one that was in a sling. "Long story, Gabe. We'll tell you later."

"You see, what I'm thinking is that they are planning to strike again, at some event where the President is to make a decision on whether to continue our mission or not. We just don't know where he's going to make this announcement." Terry said.

"And this time…" Randy started, but heard someone behind him.

"Terry! Terry!" called Billy from behind, "Look what I found."

Gabe watched as Terry and Randy looked the gun over. Standing back with Brian, Gabe decided that this was something they had been solving for quite some time, so he was going to stay out, until his entrance was necessary.

Randy looked at Gabe, "A nine millimeter handgun. I'll take this down to the forensics lab."

Gabe nodded, but Terry spoke, "Billy, Brian, excuse us for a minute please."

Billy and Brian walked out of hearing range while Terry and Gabe whispered to each other. "Man," Billy told Brian, "It went off in the hall. It could've killed someone."

Gabe took a step back from Terry, "I had suspicions from the beginning," He looked at Billy and Brian, "Hey," he called out, "Billy, meet us on the Command Arena." As Billy walked off, Gabe noted before heading off himself, "It's time to resort to T5B methods," He took Terry's walkie-talkie off his belt clip and spoke into it, "Meghan Overbay, meet me in my quarters. Gabe out." As he lowered the walkie-talkie, he told Brian and Terry, "Come on, guys. It's time we kicked some major booty."

A few minutes later, Meghan and Terry walked out of the elevator to the Command Arena. They did not have a happy look on their face, and was walking faster than normal, almost storming out of the elevator. This, in turn, drew stares from everyone. Terry walked to the Captain's Chair, and Meghan walked over to Stacey Norton's station. She had been busy on her control panel to even notice that Terry and Meghan had walked onto the Arena.

Meghan swung Stacey's chair around and punched Stacey in the face, sending her off her chair and to the floor in a hurry. Stacey immediately scooted backward, toward the viewer.

Stacey noticed that Terry raised one hand, signaling for her fellow officers to stay put, for they had stood up in defense of her. They all hesitantly sat back down, itching to get back up.

"What's going on?" she faltered, holding her busted lip.

"Get up, bitch," Meghan ordered, walking toward Stacey.

Stacey tried to scoot back some more, not attempting to get back up, but Meghan wouldn't take no for an answer. "Get up, you whore. GET UP!" She then grabbed Stacey by the uniform shirt, picked her up, and shoved her in to the television monitor. An instant later, she hit the television and bounced back to the floor with a thud. Meghan had started walking to her as she fell to the floor, and suddenly without warning, kicked her in the face, sending a couple of Stacey's teeth sliding across the floor. Terry and Billy grimaced. Only tears came from Stacey, wondering what just happened.

Gabe walked out of the elevator with Brian, who both still were in the scraggily clothing they were in when they were flashed aboard. "Hey! What's going on here?" Gabe demanded out loud.

Everyone's attention turned to Gabe, "GABE!" Stacey yelled through blood and spitting it up in the process. She ran over to Gabe and hugged him. Gabe was shocked at the moment, not knowing whether to hug her back. Gabe gave her a couple of pats on the back, and then pushed her off him slightly and studied her face. "Who did this to you?" he asked, touching her face softly.

Stacey turned around and pointed to Meghan, as if she was a scared child.

"Come on Stacey, not Meghan," He looked at Meghan, and the look on her face told him that she did, in fact, do that to Stacey, and was proud of it. "Okay, here," He helped Stacey to the front of the Command Arena where she first started out. Meghan inched back little by little as they closed in on her. "What's the matter, Meghan? Are you jealous of what Stacey and I got going on here or something?"

Meghan stared at him, and then spoke, "First of all, it's unprofessional for a commanding officer to have an affair with a subordinate, and second, but most importantly, we're divorced, remember?"

"Well, yeah," Gabe agreed, "but you have always been real possessive, even hurting people when they got in your way, so to speak." He looked at Stacey, and caressed her face with his hand, "Oh, don't worry, Stacey. We'll get that patched right up and have you feeling and looking better in no time," he turned to Meghan, "Bad Meghan!" He said, pointing a finger at her as if she was a bad pet that peed on the living room floor.

Terry smiled at Gabe's comments, 'Gabe sure had a way with words,' Terry thought.

Gabe gave Stacey a little kiss on her lips, careful to not hurt her, and then put her face onto his shoulder, comforting her. Caressing her hair,

Gabe said, "Besides, it's not like you set me up and sent me to prison or anything."

Stacey, who had her face buried in Gabe's shoulder, suddenly lifted her head back up and took a step back.

"There's no way out, Stacey. You messed up on your own," Gabe said in the most sarcastic voice he could come up with. He then wiped the little bit of blood her got from her when he kissed her.

She stepped back more and leaned her back against the television. "How?" she asked in a scared voice.

Randy stood up and took a step forward, "Number one, you were ordered to take over Terry's station when we were attacked after supposedly opening fire on the President's Convoy, but you left to follow Josh. Coincidentally, you two were knocked out on Deck C, which not-so-shockingly is the same deck as our Flash Technology Room. Around the time you two went missing on Deck C, Flash Technology was used."

Terry stood up from the captain's chair. "Number two, you were in a daze when we were talking about the weapon used to kill President Fischer. I then asked you what type of weapon was used, and you responded that it was a nine millimeter handgun. We had never known what type of gun was used until that point."

"And why in the world would you ask if an invisible ship was possible? We are using the cloak right now and you were already aware of the fact of the existence of the T5B cloak." Billy said.

"But your biggest mistake was near the beginning of the mission, right before the attack," Gabe said, this time in a detective-type voice, "My conversation; it was used against me in the trial."

"And guess who was in the doorway when Gabe made those comments?" Randy rhetorically asked.

Stacey looked around for some kind of support. She knew she wouldn't get any from T5B and Company, but perhaps her own shipmates. She glanced at every member of her fellow Marines, including Privates Zeron and Curtis, but all she got from any one of them was an apologetic look and nod.

"You know, I could've died out there and Brian did, in fact, come in close contact with death," Gabe said, trying to establish some kind of guilt trip. "I don't know about you, but if I did something like that, I would feel bad about assisting in the murder of my Commander in Chief, then at least four other people, me and Brian included. Do you even have a conscience?"

"So tell us," Lauren said, walking forward, "Were you the one in the greenhouse, because you were nowhere to be found at the time of the shooting in the greenhouse?"

Stacey knew she wasn't going to get any sympathy anymore after the evidence piled up against her, so she changed attitudes. She took one step forward, "You can't prove anything." She stuck her nose up in the air, as if was too snobby and good for them.

"The modified recording should be sufficient evidence at the moment," Gabe responded. He looked at Lauren, "Contact Josh on his personal notepad communicator."

Lauren turned the other way and went back to her station.

Gabe pulled Stacey by the arm away from the television and brought her close to him; so close their faces were merely inches from each other. "I liked you, I really did. The only problem I think we would have before continuing our relationship is getting over the little part where you tried to have me killed. Let's see: would you do that to me? Oh wait, you already did. I'm not one to hold a grudge, but I think this qualifies as an exception." He had whispered to her the entire time. Tears trickled down her cheeks.

Lauren looked up from her station, "I have him."

Gabe looked to the viewer, seeing a surprised look on Josh's face. "Well, Gabe, nice to see you alive." Josh said. Since there was a delay, they had to pause a few seconds to let the message get through. When anyone talked to anyone else on the monitor, the broadcast on both sides appeared as if they were watching a webcam. This was due to the enormous distance the broadcast had to travel through space.

Gabe quickly gave Stacey a soft, tender kiss on the lips one last time, and then put his open palm on her face, covering it. Quickly after doing so, he gave her a shove to move her away from him. She stumbled a few steps back, holding her mouth.

Gabe faced Josh while rubbing his now bloody palm on his pants, "Nice to see you, too. You do know that you risk arrest by speaking to us, right?"

"Que? No comprende. En espanol, por favor!" Josh said, cupping his ears. Josh had told him that he couldn't understand, and then asked him to speak back in Spanish.

Gabe understood, and spoke back in Spanish, knowing that if Amaya, Rustin or anyone else were listening, they wouldn't understand them right away. The language variance would throw them off, Gabe hoped. "La conferencia de prensa. ¿Dónde se va a celebrar?" He asked where the press conference was going to be held.

Josh looked at Gabe, giving him a look that said that he was sworn to secrecy. After a moment, though, Josh smiled, and then spoke in Spanish again, quoting the late Tejana singer Selena Quintanilla Perez, "No quiero saber. Tu robaste mi corazón!" Her words translate to '*I don't want to know. You stole my heart.*'

Gabe couldn't help but laugh out loud, but he then tried another tactic; surely Josh was going to help him. "Creemos que están planeando atacar de nuevo." He said that his he and his friends thought that the conspirators were going to kill again.

Josh paused a second, and then responded, "In MetLife Stadium."

"Gracias, Josh, y te amo también, Bebe."

Josh shook his head at Gabe stating that he loved him and called him Baby. He then took one glance at Gabe, and then looked to Stacey, and then back to Gabe.

Gabe explained himself, switching back to English, "You see, Josh, Stacey was just telling us about how her and her friends set us all up for murder, treason, and conspiracy."

Josh nodded, and asked, "So that's how it all went down when we supposedly fired on President Fischer?"

Gabe asked while nodding to signify a yes, "Do you recall that knot you had on your head?"

"Yeah, and it better *not* happen again, you jerk!" Josh immediately said, rubbing the back of his head.

Laughing at Josh's comments, Gabe continued, "Well, Josh, according to Randy, Stacey barely even had a little bruise on the back of her. I guess she couldn't hit herself that hard from behind."

Josh nodded his head, finally understanding, "Well, I have to go. I have been under surveillance since I left the trial and back on Earth."

"I see your point, Josh, and thank you. And you know nothing, remember that."

"*I CAN'T HEAR YOU! YOU'RE BREAKING UP!*" Josh screamed, pretending to mess with the connection settings on his notepad computer and pushing random buttons.

"Exactly. This never happened." Gabe stated.

With that, Josh cut the transmission.

Gabe walked around to Terry and got something that was latched to Terry's belt. He started walking back to Stacey and opened the casing. Stacey stepped a few steps back, but realized Meghan was blocking the other way. She immediately recognized the taser gun when Gabe finally pulled it out and tossed the casing aside.

"You see, Stacey," Gabe said, "I can't hit a girl. It's just me; I can't do it. But believe you me, I sure as hell can stun one when I realize that my life would, or could've been, in danger. And with one million volts of electricity in one shot, you're bound to get knocked down on the first shot."

"Please," Stacey pleaded, her voice changing like she was going to cry. "Gabe, don't," she held up her hand, an instinctive reaction to block.

"You will tell me what I need to know," Gabe ordered her.

"Anything. What do you want to know?" Stacey asked.

"Well, you are cooperative now. First, we couldn't prove anything, and now you're telling us what we need to know."

"Don't hurt me, Gabe, please." Stacey kept pleading. Her voice chirped and cracked throughout her sentences, as she was in true fear for her well-being.

"Okay, question one. Who's the top dog out there in charge of this conspiracy?"

She didn't hesitate to respond, "General Cue. He coordinated the whole thing. He has the schematics to your cloak."

"Simple enough. Is Amaya or Rustin involved?"

"What?" She asked.

Gabe hit the power button, making it cackle with electricity. "Just what I said, Stacey," Gabe said more forcefully, "Is, Amaya, or, Rustin, involved?" He slowed his sentence intentionally.

"Gabe, NO!" she again tried to plead with Gabe. "You asked me once, 'do you have a conscience?'"

"But I'm mucho loco at the moment." Gabe said immediately, making the taser pop again with electricity.

Randy stepped forward and interrupted the conversation, "I think that's enough Spanish for now. I'm sure the readers are sick of that crap already."

Gabe smirked at Randy, and then took one step toward Stacey, and she took one back. "I do have a conscience, Stacey, but at this point, I am mad because I was set up for murder, thrown in prison in the effing boonies in a snake and quicksand infested jungle, and left to die. So now *answer me!*" Gabe ordered.

"All right, all right. As far as I know, it's General Cue. I'm not privy to that information."

"I asked who else?" Gabe said.

"Just him," Stacey said quickly, glancing around.

Gabe hit the switch on the taser again, this time closer to her. The loud popping noise made everyone on the Command Arena jump in reaction.

"Okay, okay. Admiral Casey Rustin, and that's all I know. They are the lead conspirers, other than who knows who that's working for them."

"Meghan," Gabe said without explanation. Stacey turned around to see what Meghan would do, but instead was met with a fist. She spun around and fell to the deck and was instantly knocked out, caused by the perfectly timed and placed shot by Meghan. Meghan then kicked her in the ribs as if she lightly punted a soccer ball, and then walked away to her station.

Gabe chuckled and shook his head, "You see, I can't even use a taser on a girl; I am too soft." He grounded the taser on the metal floors and then tossed it to Terry, "I would like to, though," he finished.

"What do you think we should do with her?" Lauren asked.

"Send her to your jungle," Terry smiled as he put the taser back on his belt.

"Unfortunately," Brian stepped in, "the whole place went ka-blewy, so I don't think that's an option."

"Oh, she will go to prison, just not that one," Randy offered.

"Well, I think that first things should be first," Gabe said, "It's time to shower and get cleaned up," Gabe walked toward the elevator, followed by Brian. He paused at the elevator, thinking for a second. "Meghan, see to it she's locked in her quarters."

Meghan smiled, silently letting Gabe know that it was going to be a fun thing for her to do.

"Private Curtis," Gabe continued, "set course for the space station, maximum speed. Randy get the crew ready for battle stations. Terry, Brian, meet me in my quarters in a half hour, and Lauren, would you have sex with me?"

"What?" Lauren asked, shocked and confused.

Everyone laughed out loud and Gabe's random out-of-the-blue joke.

"Aw, come on," Gabe said, "it's be the best five seconds of your life… ever." Gabe said, and then disappeared into the elevator.

CHAPTER 11

- - - - - E N D   G A M E - - - - -

Gabe, in properly straightened tie and military uniform with the others, walked down the hallway on Deck E, accompanied by Brian and Terry.

"These ties suck, dude," Terry said.

"I know, but we need to make a second first impression with Captain Porter." Gabe replied. Only moments later, they arrived at a door where security guards were posts. "Let us in," Gabe said. It only took seconds for security to punch a few codes into the wall panel and the doors to open.

Captain Porter was sitting on a loveseat reading a book. She glanced up at the doors when they opened, revealing Gabe, Terry and Brian.

"Looks like the captain lives luxurious," Brian said, referring to the huge size of the room compared to the small, cramped quarters of everyone else.

"It's called a Captain's Suite, jerk," Porter said instantly and without hesitation.

"Captain Kirk," Gabe interrupted, "we need to talk."

"You know what, you egotistical jerk, we do, but this time you being the one locked up like a rabid animal," she snapped at him. She continued, annoyed at Gabe's sarcasm, "and I am *NOT* Captain Kirk!"

"Captain, Captain, there's no need to mince words," Terry said, "we came in peace."

"Locking me up didn't help your peaceful agenda, Mr. Farmer."

"It's Farran, lady," Terry corrected, frowning.

"Captain Porter," Gabe started, "We didn't come here to start an argument. We came here to propose your re-instatement on *Frontier*."

"And when we get home, I will see to it that all of you guys are behind bars." Porter informed them immediately.

"Captain, Admiral Amaya already knows the whole story," Brian stated.

"Kristina," Gabe said, "you don't mind if I call you that, do you?" He didn't wait for her permission to do so before speaking again. "Kristina, listen to me, we're facing a very real threat and we could use your help. You help us or you don't, that's your choice, but I'd much rather prefer your help."

"We're not entirely certain, but we could come under fire by either the United States or an invisible ship operated by a General Cue bent on destroying our reputation and mission," Terry informed her, "if we are correct, we will come under fire in approximately one hour or so. I think we could use a little real command experience here."

Brian chimed in, "Command experience in the military is something way different than people listening to their boss at Sonic Drive In."

"So why is it now that you want me to help?" Porter asked, "Why didn't you ask earlier?"

"Well," Brian said, "it's actually quite a long story, in more ways than one. One, it would deviate from the plotline, and two, I'll explain why we had to leave you out of this later on after we get back and exonerate ourselves."

"The point is, Captain," Gabe interrupted, "is that we need your help now. I am offering your ship back under the conditions that you make no decisions that will compromise unnecessary lives, like you did in Chapter Four of this book. I am pretty confident we can do it ourselves, but then again, a real, experienced military captain increases our odds tremendously."

"And what exactly are our odds now, Gabe?" she asked.

"Are chances of survival are pretty much zero, unless something else can be arranged," Gabe informed her.

Captain Porter stood up and stood face to face with Gabe. She started to straighten the slight crookedness of his tie, speaking at the same time, "Gabe, you have that certain cuteness about you, along with your unique sarcasm, that I think no one can resist. Why is that?" she said smiling.

"I think the real question is why everybody keeps hitting on Gabe, and not me," Terry said.

"Well," Brian corrected, "for one, I find it quite annoying. For two, it might be because he's the one who wrote this story in the first place."

"Well, are you with us, or not, Kristina?" Gabe asked, ignoring the others.

"Of course, Gabe. How could I say no to you?" Porter said in an almost seductive tone of voice, and all the while had finished straightening his tie and put her hands down to her side. Terry and Brian rolled their eyes.

Gabe nodded at Brian and Terry, who headed for the door, shaking their heads in disgust.

"Give me a few minutes," Porter informed them, "I'll join the three of you on the Command Arena."

Gabe smiled and started to walk out the door, following Terry and Brian. He hesitated at the door, and poked his head back in, "Hey, uh, Captain," he paused a second, obviously trying to think of a tactful way of saying what he was about to say, "you don't think we have time for a, uh, you know, me and you?" He smiled while he spoke and used back and forth finger motions.

Porter looked up, "You horn ball, isn't that sexual harassment?"

Gabe waved a peace sign with his fingers, "Peace out, Captain," and only a split second later, he disappeared.

"Ladies and Gentlemen, the President of the United States," the White House Press Secretary announced at the podium on field of MetLife Stadium. There was an applause and everyone stood up to honor the Commander in Chief. This event was held on the fifty yard line of MetLife Stadium because of the nationwide audience it was intended to reach, and there were more press officials and news outlets than there were at a normal press conference, making the usual press conference room too small for the use of this special press conference. Security was everywhere and more so than normal considering the nature of the event.

Cue's invisible starship, the *Stique,* was at the International Space Station. He was sitting in the command chair of his cramped Command Arena. It was tightly spaced together as it was originally intended to be a multi-pilot fighter jet in near earth orbits.

"Is there anyone or anything near this area of space?" Cue asked, pointing to a monitor that showed a position above the East Asian seaboard, specifically, North Korea.

"No, sir," said a subordinate lieutenant. "Just a few satellites in high orbit."

"Okay, destroy those satellites and make it look like North Korea shot them. Get in low earth orbit and do your thing. The *Frontier* should be coming within range shortly to this side of the Earth since the Earth's rotation should put Korea in direct line to the moon. Somewhere near the moon is the only place the *Frontier* could have been hiding."

Within seconds, the craft was above North Korea and sent out a missile. The missiles were also cloaked. In order to defeat the visible gas trail, the missiles were dropped into Earth's gravity toward North Korea. When they got above the capital, the fired up and heading straight back out into space and destroyed the satellites. The explosion from the missile itself was enough to destroy the three satellites that were near each other.

"Good," Cue said, "I think it's time to wait for the Five Brats return."

Gabe paced the Command Arena, while Captain Porter was in her chair. Everyone was at his or her assigned station, ready for the foreseeable battle with Cue and his cohorts. What was unforeseeable was when and where in orbit he would attack.

"How long do we have, Commander Farran?" Porter asked of Terry.

"About five minutes to standard Earth orbit and counting." His reply was almost instantaneous.

"That's about enough time. Defenses up, Red Alert," Gabe ordered, and a moment later, the red strobes that signified Red Alert starting blinking almost simultaneously, the sirens that accompanied Red Alert blared at a very loud level of volume.

"Lieutenant Overbay," Porter said while swiveling around to face Meghan, "Shut those damn sirens off."

In a flash, only the red strobe lights gave notice that the *Frontier* was headed into battle and everybody was required to report to their assigned battle stations.

"In coordination with NASA and other worldly space agencies, we have decided to continue our quest in finding out if Mars would be a suitable planet for all of us. There is a chosen site for everyone aboard whatever starship makes its way over there with a crew of 100 to test. It seems like the most suitable place on Mars to live on," The new President, Joe Kowalski, stated to the audience. He then turned a page on the canvas that was positioned next to him, as it revealed a map of Mars and a plan of a sort. "Over the next year, we'll be communicating with the team on Mars and get to know the planet from first-hand experience. There are also going to participate in a prototype and rudimentary construction of a building that will be the model for others to follow, should the plan be a success."

He turned the page, explaining more details of his plan.

One of the security guards assigned to stand within the aisles of the stands began walking toward the pressbox. On the way there, he picked up a briefcase that had been purposefully placed beforehand. On his way up the stairs, another security walked down to replace him, and while doing so, winked at him subtly to the point where no one else noticed.

As big as everyone had made the *Frontier* out to be, flying in space was different. Analogously, it was a proton of an atom of a grain of sand in the giant beach of space. It was only visible by telescope, cameras or some form of lenses faced in its direction. It zoomed through space toward the area in orbit directly above MetLife Stadium in Rutherford, New Jersey.

"How long until we can flash down to the stadium?" Gabe asked, this time not referring to the time it would take to proper flashing orbit.

"We have to get into synchronous Earth standard orbit above the flash destination before we attempt to flash anyone from Earth to the ship. It's only proper procedure." Private Kelly Curtis responded from her station.

"Slow to coasting speed and cut the engines. We'll use maneuvering thrusters. Prepare for synchronous orbit.

"Aye, Captain," Curtis responded and then turned back to her console.

As the ship cut the engines and allowed gravity and intertia take over, the viewer came on and showed the space station nearby and the eastern seaboard of the United States in the distance, surrounded by the blue globe dotted and painted with clouds as a background. It was only a minute or two before they settled into orbit around their location and warned the world of an upcoming cconspiracy plot.

Curtis turned back around to face Porter again, "Uh, Captain, I'm receiving data showing debris from various satellites and a distress call from the United Stations Space Station."

Porter stood up and stepped forward, "Open transmissions." After Curtis confirmed that they were online, Porter spoke, "United Nations Space Station, come in please. We've received your distress call."

Terry turned around also, giving her some information of his own, "Life signs show three human bodies aboard, but they do not appear to be alive as we are receiving no heat transfer data from their life signs."

Crossing one arm and resting the elbow of her other on it, she placed her hand, index finger up, on her chin, contemplating the situation.

Gabe stepped forward to stand right next to Porter and tried this time, "United Nations Space Station, come in please. We are here to assist."

As if timing was precise, a missile appeared on their viewer and crashed into the space station. As with any spatial explosion, the station disintegrated into pieces, consumed by a fireball and winced out moments later, leaving only crackling debris, similar to a dying firecracker fuse.

Before anyone could contemplate on what just happened, the speakers responded, but not with the response anyone expected, "Romero, peek a boo. I can see you."

Gabe stepped forward, almost as if he had rehearsed, turning his left ear to the speakers, instantly recognizing the voice, "Q!" He said slowly.

Randy stood up and took a step toward Gabe, "Uh, Gabe?"

Gabe turned to look at Randy, "What?"

"It's *C, U, E,* as in cue ball, not *Q,* the letter of the alphabet, all right?" Randy whispered out loud, spelling it out for him.

"Oh, right. Let's try that again," and with that, Gabe took another step forward, "Cue!" He said slowly.

"It is I, Mr. Romero. I see that it's going to be unfortunate for you to fight me. But on the bright side, at least the most wanted terrorist and prison escapee in United States history will be abolished for good and I will be the feel-good hero of the day."

Gabe glanced at Terry as he slid his hand across his throat to signal for a communications block, and stepped in Randy's direction, "Randy, this is our big chance to find out who has that bad indigestion and letting out all that gas."

A moment later, the ship lurched. The red alert sirens that were silenced earlier blared loudly. "Gabe, one missile hit at one hundred eighty degrees mark port," Lauren informed him.

"Magnetic armor holding," Meghan added.

Gabe ran over to Terry, putting his arm around Terry, "Any ideas, buddy?"

Terry thought quickly, trying to come up with a plan, "Perhaps an antimatter discharge directly ahead might disrupt his cloaking field long enough for us to lock onto him."

The ship lurched backward this time, causing Gabe to let go of Terry and stumble. Gabe glanced at Meghan, but received a response from Billy over the intercom. "Armor at ninety percent."

Gabe turned back to Terry, "In English, Commander."

"Photon torpedo," Terry said immediately.

Gabe walked away from him, crossing his hands behind his back. "Load torpedo bays," he started, "prepare to fire at my command."

"Uh, Gabe," Porter interrupted, "We don't have any torpedoes."

Gabe turned around and grimaced, "Don't tell me: Tuesday?"

"Well, actually, we don't have torpedoes, and that includes photon torpedoes. This isn't Star Trek; we carry missiles. And just *what the hell* does Tuesday have anything to do with this?"

"*Terry...*" Gabe turned toward Terry, squinting at him while ignoring Porter.

"Well, hell, it sounded good in the movie," Terry said, "and you were the one who agreed to it, you moron."

Cue's ship fired another missile, and it flew to the *Frontier*'s top front end and exploded, scorching the ship while sending it on an instant downward turn.

"Whoa!" Gabe said, gripping a console, like everyone else, to keep from falling.

"Gabe!" Terry called out, "it might be possible to simulate a torpedo blast by modifying the main deflector. That might break his cloak, even if just for a little bit."

Gabe made no move to make an order "Terry," he explained slowly, "as much as I like playing battle of the wits here, I must inform you that we are in real danger right now. I think you have forgotten that there is no such thing as photon torpedoes."

Porter rolled her eyes, wondering how T5B managed to get anything done as they kept making jokes in the light of very real danger and peril. Lives, including theirs, were at risk and they were cracking jokes. But in some odd irony, their relationship between one another allowed for and needed that kind of sarcasm to get things done.

Terry turned away from Gabe and went back to his monitor and spoke, smiling, "All right. Give me a second and I'll have a plan for you."

Porter walked over to the captain's chair and grabbed her walkie-talkie, "Billy Fonder, what do we know about General Cue's cloak?"

After a few seconds of impatient waiting, Billy explained, "Well, nothing much, Captain. If it's modelled after or anything similar to T5B's, then…" he was cut off, and why he was cut off came an instant later.

The ship rocked hard this time, sending everyone off his or her feet or chair, almost like a snow globe being shaken. Consoled exploded near Lauren and Meghan. Luckily, everyone, including Lauren and Meghan, had been knocked out of their chair.

After a few moments, everybody was back up and where they were supposed to be, hoping that Gabe, or someone, would come up with a plan quickly in time to save their lives.

"T5B's cloak shouldn't even be used anymore because of defective inducer coils in the device. Those coils were defective since the very beginning and should either be redesigned or replaced with a similar technology." Randy spoke out.

Porter spoke to Billy again, re-establishing contact, "Commander Fonder, suppose all cloaks have these inducer coils Randy is talking about. Are they subceptible to some kind of inverse radio or magnetic pulse?"

"Perhaps," Billy said, "if we activate an inverse radio pulse and target the coils, it might reset their cloaking devie and we could lock on to them."

"Terry," Gabe ordered, "lock onto those inducer coils!"

Terry stood up from his station and walked over to another console and started pushing buttons. A moment later, Terry turned around, and spoke, "Ready when you...". He was interrupted by the very console he was working with as it exploded into a shower of sparks, sending debris in outward directions. Terry instinctively covered his head with his hands and tried to get away but some of the debris had hit him in the back of the knee, causing him to stumble and fall forward.

The exploding console set off a domino effect of exploding consoles and sconces throughout the Command Arena. Instantly, everyone jumped out of his or her chair or station and dove to the deck. Smoke started to fumigate the Arena, and several more lights shattered and burst, sending shards of broken glass in every direction.

Billy talked to the Command Arena, "Armor collapsing," he said over the walkie-talkies from a station in the engine room. Above his console was a computer display from the *Frontier*, and line around the ship representing the armor encircled it. It was blinking off and on.

On the Command Arena, any remaining working lights continued to shatter as the electrical surge reached them. It sent the Command Arena in a state of red-darkness. The only remaining lights were the red strobing lights.

"Emergency lights," Porter ordered, and moments later, four small light figures embedded in the wall lit up, flickering off and on and a slow, steady pace.

Terry had already stood back up, and called out, "I'm okay. So much for that pulse; we need a new plan."

Billy's voice came on the walkie-talkies again, and this time he did his Scotty from Star Trek imitation, complete with the fake accent. "We just can't handle it, Captain! We… just… can't… handle… it!" he said as loud as he could without screaming.

The security guard that had left his post in the stadium continued walking down a hallway in the pressbox. Moments later, he got a door marked "PRIVATE" as it was a private suite for those with VIP tickets to events. He swiped his badge on the door reader and walked in the room. He closed the door and entered a security code into the door panel, locking it.

He then went to the window, which was facing the football field. He then set his briefcase on a table nearby and began assembling a sniper rifle.

President Kowalski was speaking at this time. "The nations of the world must understand that this is not a decision that comes lightly. We have an obligation to our race and we must all cooperate together. I hope this press conference we are having today will prove to the world that not all United States citizens are like the rogue ones aboard *Frontier*."

Admiral Amaya, sitting in the front row, raised an eyebrow, unsure how to react to the comments made by Kowalski. Perhaps it was just his way of words, Amaya thought.

"Gabe!" Randy called out, "Remember Atomic Missile Alpha One?"

"*Oh, how could I forget?*" Gabe immediately responded, narrowing his eyes, looking at Porter in the process.

"We won't survive many more hits," Private Curtis informed from her station.

The speakers came on again, showing that Cue opened transmissions, "Oh, Mr. Romero?"

Gabe looked up, "What?"

"Face it, I am the poo, so you better take a good whiff."

"Yeah, I could've told you that you smelled like crap." Gabe snapped back.

On Cue's Command Arena, Cue frowned. Apparently, Gabe was little quicker when it came to a battle of the wits, and turned his catchy line back on him. However unprofessional his remarks were, he was trying to insult Gabe by using a juvenile smart remark. He turned to his weapons officer and signaled for another missile.

"Gabe!" Randy snapped, "Atomic Missile Alpha One. We could jury-rig the warhead to explode in a spherical detonation. If we get it to explode near his ship, it will destroy him. A cloak like T5B's takes tremendous energy and a shockwave that big will surely destroy the ship."

"What about this ship?" Gabe asked.

Porter intervened on the conversation, "I'm not sure. This ship was designed to survive a nuclear blast without radiation leaking into the ship, but the damage we've suffered and no armor on the ship, we might not survive as well."

Gabe thought for a moment, but his thoughts were interrupted by a soft lurch of the ship. He looked up at Terry.

As if he already knew Gabe's question, Terry responded, "I'm sending out buoys to mock the readings of our ship. It's allowing us to dodge Cue's missiles, but only for the time being."

Porter spoke as Gabe gave Terry a nod of approval, "Gabe, you and Randy get that warhead ready to fire. Private Curtis, you, Meghan, Lauren, Zeron, and Brian get down to MetLife and warn them of the impending danger. Carry a gun, knife, or whatever you have to do, to stop them. Terry, Billy and I will send Cue to hell."

"How about I stay here, Captain, and you go? You have more pull with security down there than we do." Gabe asked.

"Captain goes down with her ship, remember?" she stated nonchalantly.

Gabe smiled, understand the familiar adage. He was still intent on staying aboard the *Frontier.* He grabbed walkie-talkie and spoke into it, "Billy, meet Randy in Missile Control. I'll help here."

Porter thought only for a second, and then she responded in her walkie-talkie, "Go ahead."

A few seconds later, everyone disappeared into the elevator, leaving Porter, Terry and Gabe behind alone.

"Well, Terry, I love you, man." Gabe said with a fake sniffle. He rubbed his eyes as if he was fixing to cry.

"No, you don't." Terry said smiling, and the ship lurched again, signifying the buoys were still working.

"I know, but I thought it sounded good," Gabe said and headed over to Meghan's former station and started inputting commands. "In a few minutes we might not survive the blast, Captain. It has been an honor, Kristina, just in case I don't get the chance to say it later."

"No, Gabe, the honor is all mine." Porter responded with a most sincere voice.

"Cry havoc," Cue's voice said over the speaker, "and let slip the dogs of war."

"Oh, God," Gabe said, "shut the hell up, already."

At that moment they were surrounded again by a series of explosions from the rest of the working consoles. Fire was sporadic across the Arena, following the console explosions and electrical surges. Smoke filled the Command Arena. The ship took a direct hit to the Command Arena with a missile, and began a slow downward descent to Earth.

Brian, Meghan, Lauren, Privates Curtis and Zeron, among a few others, flashed directly to the hallway in MetLife Stadium. They studied their surroundings for a moment, and then Brian motioned with a waving hand, "This way!"

The started walking, and within moments came upon an entrance to the football stadium seats and field. Brian turned to face Curtis and Zeron, "Check around the stadium seating. Both Zeron and Curtis, along with their additional coworkers, spanned out in opposite directions, determined to span the seating area. Brian, Lauren and Meghan started running up the bleachers and got to the pressbox, but were stopped by a security guard.

"Hold it there, guys. I can't let you in." The security told them.

Quicker than the guard could see or react, Brian pulled a pocket knife and held it to the guard's throat, "Let us in!"

The guard handed Meghan his security clearance card as Lauren took his pistols from him. Brian then lowered his knife, put it in his pocket, and without warning, he elbowed the guard to the jaw, knocking him out. "Go search these rooms. I'll go save the president."

As Meghan and Lauren disappeared into the pressbox, Brian ran down the stairs and onto the field. Admiral Amaya was now on stage, speaking.

"Within three years of their landing and colonization on Mars, they will be scheduled to head back to Earth, leaving all their supplies and equipment set up for future generations of explorers."

While the noise in the stadium was mostly contained to the bleachers, the press conference went on as normal. What interrupted the conference, though, was Brian's intrusion onto the field where the important political figures and news outlets were located.

Amaya had stopped talking as he noticed Brian a few military personnel chasing him. One guard was able to step in front of Brian a few meters away, but quickly, Brian dove to the ground and rolled, tripping the guard over him and sending the guard into the others that had been chasing him. Smoothly, Brian had got back up and continued running toward Amaya.

Another officer stepped in front of Brian, but instantly, and instead of rolling, Brian grabbed his outstretched arm and used it to seemingly defy gravity and used it to run upward onto a couple of chair backs. Using the momentum, his body was still headed to the Admiral, holding on the Secret Service guard. Once the momentum placed him in the direction of Amaya, he let his body fall to the ground, back first, still holding on the guard's arm. The guard went down with him, but once Brian landed, he used his legs and feet to catapult the guard into the air and away from him.

Getting up, he stopped, realizing he caught everyone's attention. Breathing hard, he yelled, "Admiral Amaya, sir! we have learned of a possible assassination attempt at this…" He didn't have time to explain as a gunshot rang out. Admiral Amaya went down.

Randy and Billy were hurrying to finish the missile in Missile Control. It was almost like they were surgeons because the missile was placed on stretcher or bed of sorts while they operated on the electronics of the warhead.

While they were doing so, the speakers came on again, indicating that someone was fixing to talk again, "Cry woe, distruction, ruin and decay. The worst is death. And Death will have this day." It was Cue's voice quoting some unknown lyric, poem, or story that seemed relevant to the situation at hand.

"I really wish this guy would shut, the, hell, up!" Bill said, emphasizing his language.

Randy put his computer tablet down beside the missile and pulled his walkie-talkie, "Randy to Porter!" He used his free hand to grab the overhead straps and help Billy hook them onto the missile. The purpose of this strap was to lift the missile and place onto the ramps that fed the missile tubes.

He got no response, he tried another person. "Randy to Gabe, come in please," he said harsher. He glanced at Billy, who was finishing loading the warhead onto the ramp.

The Command Arena was engulfed in heavy smoke. The lights that were signifying Red Alert were no longer functioning, so the only visibility around was of the flames out of several stations. On the back of the Arena, a computer screen flashed, "Air Pressure

Alert!" A slight whining sound echoed throughout the Arena, as if air was escaping from a tiny hole in a newly inflated tire that ran over a nail.

A hand gripped Meghan's console, and Gabe appeared. His walkie-talkie still chirped. "Randy to Gabe, I repeat, come in please."

After Gabe steadied himself on the console, he looked around as he grabbed his own walkie-talkie. Breathing hard, he replied to Randy's calls, "Randy, I'm here."

Instantly, Randy responded, "Atomic Missile Alpha One programmed and ready to fire at your command."

"What Randy and I have done is use this computer tablet to program the missile to find a pattern within the origin of all of the missiles fired and triangulate a guessing point at where Cue might be next." Billy added to the conversation, "Even if he moves in time, space is very giant, and it's not like we can move very fast in outer space in the span of only a few seconds."

"Randy, Billy," Gabe said, breathing harder this time, "get to a flash room and get everyone off the ship and onto the grounds of MetLife Stadium. We will fire that missile from here."

"What about you?" Randy asked.

"Don't worry about us, Randy. Save the others. That's our original mission as a group: to save and help others, even if we or the ship doesn't survive in the process, so all of you, get the hell out of here! No time."

Gabe coughed and before Billy or Randy could counter a response, Gabe turned off his walkie-talkie and dropped it to the deck.

He crawled a little ways and found Porter lying face down near the Captain's Chair. He turned her over, and found she was scorched everywhere, and some of her clothes were burned. "Oh, God, please don't die." He whimpered.

Porter coughed, as Gabe held her neck to support her head. She opened her eyes and looked at Gabe, "Gabe," she said, voice hoarse.

"Shhh, you're gonna be all right," Gabe said reassuringly.

"No, I'm not," Porter said, couhing up blood. "Do just one thing for me, please?"

"What's that?" Gabe asked, a tear trickling down his cheek.

"Don't let him win… just, don't let, him, win." She took only a couple more breaths, and then she fell unconscious. Gabe already knew that she just didn't pass out. He kissed her forehead, laid her head down softly, and then took his military jacket and covered her up in it as if he was tucking his child into bed at night after a bedtime story.

"I won't, Kristina, I won't," Gabe promised softly as if she could still hear him. Using his hands to search the floor as if he lost a contact lens, he searched frantically for Terry. He was fortunate to find Terry knocked out only about five meters away. As he shook Terry, Terry regained his senses and sat up after a few moments.

"Terry," Gabe coughed, "fire that damn missile because I sure don't know how."

Once Terry caught his breath, he crawled to the nearest working station and started inputting commands.

Billy looked at Randy, unsure on what to do. Randy then ordered, "Well, you heard him. We have a mission to complete. We just have to input this final number sequence into the tablet and the missile is armed. Then we flash everyone aboard this ship out of here." They then ran down to the platform so they could to the Flash Technology Room.

For some reason, the bullet had missed Amaya and struck the marble in the podium. Almost in the center was a lone bullet, forever to be embedded in the marble, originally intended to kill the Admiral. At the same time the bullet had struck the marble, the pressbox glass windows from the private suite had shattered.

After the initial shock of the failed assassination attempt passed, everyone looked up to the broken suite's window. There stood Meghan and Lauren, holding their pistols up in the air and standing back to back, as if they were posing for some movie poster designed for two leading women to be heroines. Meghan blew on her pistol tip as if it was smoking and she made a kill shot in the old west.

Guards and other men grabbed Brian, as if to arrest him, but Amaya interrupted, "Hold on, gentlemen. What is the meaning of this, Commander Rendetti?"

"Just give us a few minutes, sir, and I'm sure Gabe will explain the whole situation." Brian countered.

Once Terry was able to gain complete access to the console, he told Gabe, "Okay, this should take only a few seconds."

A male computer activated voice came over the speaker, "Ship implosion in one minute."

Randy looked up toward the speakers. He and Billy were in a Flash Room ready to send everyone back to Earth.

"So," Billy asked, "where are we sending everyone?"

"To MetLife parking lot, and then sort them out later. For us, we're going directly to center field ourselves."

After a few more seconds, they flashed from their spots and off of the *Frontier.*

"Ready and able," Terry confirmed.

Gabe leaned forward, "Fire."

Terry pushed the button to send the missile out of the ship.

On the front tip of the *Frontier* was a missile bay, the only one other than the one on the back tip of the ship. It took only a few seconds for the missile to fly out of the bay and into space.

Cue stood up from his chair aboard his ship, "What's this?"

"It appears the *Frontier* is trying one, last desperate attempt at firing on us." His weapons officer said, "it appears to be going in circles."

"Not anymore," Cue said, pointing to the viewer. The missile came to a stop directly ahead of them. He turned to his helm officer, "Get us out of here!" he screamed.

The convoy made an instant 180 degree turn and started to head away from the missile.

"Ship implosion in fifteen seconds," the computer voice told Gabe and Terry.

"Detonate," Gabe ordered Terry, and Terry complied by hitting another button. A split second later, the missile exploded, sending a spherical three-dimensional fireball and shockwave in all directions..

It took only a couple of seconds to reach Cue's ship, and when it did, his ship exploded instaneously, caused by what looked like a ball of fire that grew in space.

"Warning: Ship implosion in ten seconds. Collision in ten seconds." The computer warned.

"Well, Terry, all this," Gabe said, trying to think of an appropriate word, "was fun." Unlike earlier when he spoke to Terry, a real tear trickled down his cheek. He put a friendly hand on Terry's shoulder.

"Oh yes," Terry said with an almost-sad look on his face. He looked up to Gabe, and placed his left hand on top of Gabe's hand that was on his shoulder, "It sure was, Gabe."

Then they both braced themselves for what was surely the last few seconds of their lives.

The shockwave hit the *Frontier* from the underside and sent the ship flying upwards at incredible speeds. Along the way, the ship tore apart from bow to stern, and engulfed itself into a fireball that winced out moments later by the vacuum of space. Silenced loomed in the empty vacuum and debris from the United Nations Space Station, the *Stique,* the destroyed satellites, and the *Frontier,* scattered like a group of fireflies in a forest, each with their own distinctive blink as the metals from all the ships and stations scattered like a broken mosaic.

Billy and Randy appeared in the middle of the field at MetLife Stadium. Instantly, news crews focused their attention onto the duo who appeared out of nowhere.

Billy asked Randy, ignoring the cameras and news crews, "Did you save Gabe and Terry?"

Randy shrugged and a tear streamed down his face. Billy covered his mouth with his hand, and took a step back, stumbling. He caught himself on a chair that was behind him, and steadied himself, "Oh, no..." he said, not being able to say anything else.

CHAPTER 12

- - - - - F I N A L I T Y - - - - -

Brian ran to Admiral Amaya on stage to make sure he was safe. While visually inspecting the admiral, Amaya asked, "What is the meaning of all of this?"

Again, timing was precise and Brian's walkie-talkie chirped with Meghan's voice, "Brian, we killed the would-be assassin."

Brian reached for his walkie-talkie but Amaya took it from his hand, "Lieutenant Overbay, there better be a good explanation for this."

It was Lauren's turn to talk, "Admiral Amaya, sir, we burst in the door just in time as he was aiming in your direction. Instinctively, we fired to save your life. An instant before we shot, he was pulling the trigger, so our shot reached him in time for him to miss."

"You still have explained anything, Lieutenant Stone." Amaya said impatiently.

"Admiral, if you'd have some freaking patience and quit interrupting us, we'd tell you," Meghan spoke this time, "there was an attempt on your life and an attempt to compromise this mission's success. The assassin we have shot up here in the pressbox is Admiral Casey Rustin."

The entire audience heaved a heavy sigh in unison at the revelation.

It was at that instant, what appeared to be camera flashes caught everyone's attention, and Gabe and Brian appeared about ten feet away from Billy and Randy.

Billy looked in awe as he was shocked to see them alive. "How…" he managed to utter.

Randy smiled, "Because, we were interrupted and you didn't let me finish. I took an educated guess and timed their response times to detonation of the missile and set the auto-flash sequencer to capture them before they decided to blow themselves up."

"You bastard," Billy accused.

Gabe and Terry looked at each other, and then screamed together, "Woo-hoo! We're alive!!!" They then bumped butts and started dancing some dance they made up on the spot. The entire audience just stared at them, wondering what was going on.

Once Gabe and Terry noticed they were the main attraction to everyone's attention, they stopped. "Oops!" They said together and then pretended to straighten their hair and uniforms while whistling a random tune. They acted for a few moments as if they were innocent in all the dance and charade they performed a few seconds ago.

"Now that you two are done with your circus act, let me remind you that you are nationally televised at this moment," Admiral Amaya said into the microphone. "And also now that we have your attention, I think it's time to confess, Commander Romero."

Dusting himself off as he walked to the stage, Gabe seemed perplexed, "What do you mean, Admiral?"

"What I mean, Commander, is what is the meaning of you interrupting this world broadcast event, considering the fact you and your group are wanted for conspiracy, treason and escape?"

As he walked up the stairs, Gabe reached out his hand to take the microphone away from Amaya. He knew he had to make this speech a good one, as his face was now plastered across millions of television sets across the world.

"Well, Admiral," he started, "it's about the future. Some people are prejudice of the future and what will happen, and will even go at great lengths to keep the good of humanity from prevailing. What will happen? What are we supposed to do? How are we supposed to act? This event you were having today is the first step of many in an effort to show that humanity is ready to explore the stars, travel through space and colonize new worlds. We should work together in a worldly effort to overcome those who are bent on stopping all of us from achieving our dreams. Humanity may not be perfect, but people like us can help pave the way for a greater future."

President Kowalski walked up to Gabe and reached out his right hand, "You, sir, have restored my faith in this mission, as I am sure you have done for others as well."

"I am nothing without my friends," Gabe said modestly while pointing to his friends and accepted Kowalski's hand of friendship.

Admiral Amaya clapped in approval, and the audience followed in unison.

"Well," Gabe said while walking into a local pool hall with his friends, "At least we don't have to go to jail again."

"That's true," Brian added, "I'm kinda glad we got a full presidential pardon for all of our so-called illegal actions during our time in Brazil, and in space."

"We're all just glad to have you two back, safe and sound," Randy said.

"So, what happens now? Do we wait for a new ship to be built and then go to Mars?" Billy asked.

"Nah," Terry answered, "they will find another crew to go to Mars and we will all serve as advisors to the mission, still fulfilling our duties to them."

"Yeah," Josh finished for Terry, "President Kowalski has his hands full averting a war with North Korea because of General Cue's actions. He's in diplomatic talks as we speak."

"And this will be one of the times I sure am glad to be back home," Lauren said, "on Earth."

The bartender was already lining out the bar with glasses and filling them with the group's favorite drink of choice, Crown and Coke.

"And perhaps," Meghan said, walking up to Gabe, straightening his tie and collar for him, "we can finish where we left off."

Gabe studied her for a second, and then turned around and picked up two glasses from the bar. "To us," he said, giving her a glass and gesturing for a toast.

Terry and the others picked up their respective glasses. Terry lifted his higher and spoke, "And also, to T5B, in which I honestly believe this mission would have failed without us, but only with the assistance of our late friend, Captain Kristina Porter."

"Perhaps, the future of T5B has re-emerged from the shadows to once again fill everybody with laughter, sorrow, hate, humor and fun," Randy added.

After clinging their glasses together at once, everyone drank to the toast, knowing that even though The Five Brats had officially ended several years ago, the adventures of the new T5B were just beginning.

THE END
_____

--THE FIVE BRATS--

Printed in the United States
By Bookmasters